THIS LIFE

THIS LIFE

MY LIFE AFTER MY STROKE

JERRY PATRICK SCHELLHAMMER

authorHOUSE®

AuthorHouse™
1663 Liberty Drive
Bloomington, IN 47403
www.authorhouse.com
Phone: 1-800-839-8640

Published by AuthorHouse   05/31/2012

ISBN: 978-1-4772-0754-3 (sc)
ISBN: 978-1-4772-0753-6 (e)

Library of Congress Control Number: 2012908579

I'm sitting in my neighborhood bar drinking my favorite brew; I think it's number seven or eight. My mind isn't on the here and now, but on some thought, opinion, or sporting event else where when a flash from a camera strobe catches my attention.

I don't understand why she took my picture.

Chapter One

T here is a beginning to this story called life. I ended one aspect of life November 21<u>st</u> 2002. My new life is ongoing. Here is what happens when excess interferes with one's will to live. Granted, it's not easy to look at you and realize that you fucked up, and that you have to fix it. I know what I did before this date. I realized years before that date, when I was walking toward a county holding cell, or drunk tank, if you will, for the third time, I had a drinking problem. But, I didn't care. It's that simple. I really didn't care before November 21<u>st</u>, 2002 how I conducted my life, who my so-called friends were, and how I abused my body and mind.

All that changed this day, when heading towards a pool table to shoot a shot, where my good drinking buddy, Peter is playing pool, and where the Moose Lodge I frequent is half occupied with fellow drinking buddies, my left leg decided to suddenly and unexpectedly give out on me. There's no rhyme or reason for this, except, I suspect, some medical issue has suddenly reared its ugly head at me. Moments earlier, while I waited on Peter to shoot some lucky shots that eventually ran the table on me; I felt a queer pop inside my head I have never felt before. I somehow stagger my way to the pool table and place both my hands on the green felt covered slate table and tell Peter, "Something's not right."

"Shoot your shot," he replies. He's a tall six foot something, whereas I'm just over five and a half feet. He's that wiry sort that tends to always gets pick captain of the junior high PE flag football team; I was always picked last and had to prove my self. His Face is acne scarred and sports something of a mustache and beard; it's quite thin and he looks untrustworthy, according to my mother. Mother doesn't seem to care for my friends for some reason. Anyway, his expression suddenly changes; the lines on his face deepen with concern when he realizes I'm not kidding. "You want me to call 911?"

"Yeah, I think I'm having a stroke."

"Here, let me help you to a chair." I literally fall on him as he more or less drags me to a chair. He runs over to the phone that sits just behind the bar. There's nothing more for me to do, but wait for this life I foolishly squandered since age 19 to end. My name is Jack, and I'm an alcoholic. This is rock bottom for me. The half consumed beer that still sits on the bar is no longer important to me, nor is the smoldering generic cigarette laying in the ashtray; the half pack of smokes sitting on the bar next to the still smoldering cigarette, that I spent a fortune for, doesn't even hold importance to me at this point in my life. I'm fuckin' 44 and am too damn young to die like this.

It's a small world we occupy and word of my issues spread like a wild fire. Soon, old men come to offer their assistance while we wait for EMS to arrive. "Is everything alright Jack? Can we get you anything?"

"No, I'm okay. The paramedics are coming soon."

"I have some nitro pills."

"I'm not having a heart attack, Jim. I'm fairly convinced I'm having a stroke. I don't think it would be a good idea to take nitro." He means well, but if I'm bleeding out from my brain, like I suspect, nitro would be a death nail for me.

Two men in blue uniforms pulling a cart with oxygen bottles make their way to me. "How we doing today?"

"I seem to have lost my balance."

"Well, let's see what we can do then."

"I think I'm having a stroke," I say to them as they roll up my sweater sleeve to take my blood pressure. While blood pressure is taken the other paramedic asks me a battery of questions. "What's your name?"

"Jack."

"How many fingers am I holding?"

"5." "Sorry, just kidding. You're holding two."

"What's your birth date?"

"September 2nd, 1958."

"How old are you?"

"Is this a trick question? 44."

"Finally, who's the president?"

"George W Bush," I reply with disgust.

"BP is 169 over 110," the other paramedic states. Just then two other uniformed men show up. On their shoulder sleeves AMC Ambulance emblazoned with pride. That's damn high. No wonder I'm having a stroke. One of them places a plastic hose around my head and hooks it to my nose. I'm placed on a Gurney and taken up a short flight of stairs. The two move me outside and place me on the back of an ambulance. We're off to the nearest hospital.

If truth is stranger than fiction, than I'm in a Strange land. The ambulance travels exactly three blocks to Holy Family Hospital. I know it looks like a hospital because I've been there a couple of times. Just three or four months earlier I had my hernia repaired. It was one of those same day affairs. When I could see the building it's rectangular and about seven or eight stories high. There's an emergency entrance in the back, and a main entrance with lobby, and smiling grand motherly volunteer in some gray looking smock, sitting at an information booth. I won't be going there though. The ambulance driver calls ahead to inform the hospital my status and that I appear to be having a stroke. So I won't be seeing the smiling hostess this time.

At the emergency entrance, there's already a group of nurses and doctors waiting for me. I'm taken off the Gurney and placed on a hospital Gurney. Somebody is using very sharp scissors to cut fabric and places me in a gown. I don't know what they did with my shredded clothes. While that person did that, someone else grabbed my penis and inserted a catheter. Another places an IV on me, pricking my skin with a very sharp needle, but I don't seem to feel any pain. I can't explain that. I don't consider myself overly tolerant when it comes to pain sensations; must be the adrenaline kicking into high gear. Some other asshole is asking me the same questions the paramedics asked me at the Moose Lodge's Social Quarters. That's a funny euphemism for a bar. Sure they go there to socialize, but there's a bunch that go there to drink and nothing more. I should know I'm one of them. I'd go there to get drunk and nothing more. Then I would drive back home to Suncrest, a whole seventeen miles away, on a suspended license, no less. I'm damn lucky I never got caught.

Well, one time I did, but actually only drank one beer that night and just didn't feel like going anywhere. That was at the Wagon Wheel. I saw the State Trooper waiting for someone to leave. Like that one popular joke's punch line, I was the designated drunk. I told him I had a beer and he had me blow in the portable breathalyzer unit he pulled from his briefcase.

I blew a 0.48. I also told him I didn't have a license. I didn't tell him about the bench warrant in Benton County though. But, apparently it wasn't important enough for this trooper to waste his time with either. "It looks like you better take care of that problem in Benton County. Here's a ticket for driving on a suspended license. Since you're so close to your home, I'll let you drive the rest of the way."

Back to the here and now. I'm being sent to x-ray so CT-scan can be performed on my brain. On it, they'll find the ruptured vessel spurting blood on the right front lobe. A neurosurgeon, name Katrina Morgan, will be called in and perform the operation. So, sometime between her showing up, waiting on Mom and Dad to arrive to sign consent forms, then the prep work, and the actual surgery, the blood on my brain, acted like a poison, and not just affected my leg, but my left arm as well. I don't know if it would have made any difference. I like to think it would, but only God knows for sure. The X-ray chamber, where the CT apparatus is housed, makes a humming sound that makes me literally nauseous. It's understandable tonight because I've been drinking and hadn't eaten since lunch. But then, it's the next day, with a new cadre of technicians. One guy I'll never forget because he's such an arrogant prick; I named Dick. I don't know what his real name, but he reminds me of a particular Republican Vice President currently serving our find land.

The surgery went good, from what I heard while somewhat half conscious at two in the morning. There's a nice Frankenstein staple job on the right side of my skull where they cut in and apparently stopped the bleeding. They're also one of those nico-derm patches on my arm to prevent me from smoking ever again. That's my Mother's idea

I started smoking when I played recess with my school friends. I don't know who, but someone snuck a cigarette from their dad's cigarette pack. I took a puff, without even thinking. Dad smoked pipes regularly, and Mom would occasionally light up a Kent she had stashed in the butter drawer, next to her hearing aid batteries in the Frigidaire. I always wanted to at least try it. Once I did, I felt as if destined to smoke, like those actors on TV. I smoked intermittently, clandestinely, for eight years. Once I was legal, I smoke a pack a day, more if I drank or smoke pot. Mother harped on me not to smoke, or to quit once I became addicted.

But I digress; back to the X-ray tech named Dick. He's tall and nerdy looking and has this mommy boy whiney tone coming from him that I'm sure made the other techs and nurses' skin crawl. The doctors apparently wanted another CT scan done on me because it's not their money, it's the insurance. Now, I'm back in this room with the humming sounds emitting from its motors, I'm sure. Apparently, Dick wants to be in charge because he's a man and the other techs and nurses are women.

"Let's get this done," he commands to them. I don't know if they're actually listening to him, or just doing their job and ignoring him. They place me back on the bed and pull the halo looking thing over my head. "Now, tell him not to move!"

I don't move until I have an itch and I assume the procedure is done. "He moved! I thought I told you people to tell him not to move!"

Is he for real? "Sorry," I tell the tech. "I thought you were done."

"It's okay," she replies. I notice her tag reads Shelly. She's a cute twenty-something with short brown hair and clear skin, with bright wide smile. "Try not to move until we're done and this halo is removed." So the procedure starts all over again. The humming is making me sick. I don't know why. It must be something in my distant past. I try to hold back the urge to puke. And just as the halo is removed, and I think everything is okay, Dick comes out to supervise the nurses again. Apparently he doesn't think they're capable of placing me back on my hospital bed without his input. It comes without warning. At least last night I felt it coming and warned everyone before hand. Dick is right there, and I let him have it on his white lab coat and expensive looking slacks and black shiny shoes.

"He puked on me! Somebody get me a towel."

They ignore him and take care of me. Wiping up the vomit from my hospital gown and the floor. I guess someone threw him a towel. I'm brought back to the ICU area and a clean gown is placed on me. I can't say I'm sorry Dick got the blunt of my morning breakfast. I think he deserves everything he got.

The rest of the morning is spent with various doctors, whose faces I hadn't seen before, nor will ever see again, popping in to poke and prod me. Asking me to try and move my fingers and toes. I'm not sure what it is they're looking for, or why the majority of them are even here. It seems maybe if they put their name on the patient's record, the insurance will pay them for their time. After lunch I sleep, or at least the doctors aren't showing up. I have a personal nurse. Her name is Carol. She looks a little younger than me. She pops in to do the vitals thing and asks me if I need anything. "No, I'm fine," I reply.

There's not much more she can do for me. She has a pretty smile and beautiful blue eyes. Her hands are small and delicate. She wears those blue hospital scrubs that I'm sure are comfortable to wear; at least more comfortable than those polyester smocks the other nurses wear. I can't tell how tall she is. I guess that's not important now. Today is November 22<u>nd</u>. On this day in history, my childhood hero was shot dead in Dallas, Texas. Thank God I didn't end up that way on this most sacred anniversary. I could never forgive myself.

So here I lay on this bed in this ICU ward, alone with my thoughts. I can't say I feel sorry for myself. I can't say I feel anything right now. The day is clear and sunny. I guess, considering the date, it's quite chilly. If I weren't lying in this hospital bed, I'd be at work, picking up paper cups and depositing cigarette butts in a cup and wiping slot machines with a cloth towel. It's not a bad place to work, at the casino. It's a job that pays very little; barely enough to pay rent and make car payments on my Dodge Intrepid I financed back in March. What money is left over, I spend on getting drunk at the Wagon Wheel or Moose Lodge. I live with my parents, and had plans to move on my own within next year. Obviously that won't be happening anytime soon. What will most likely happen in my future is very much uncertain. Except, right here and right now, I have to turn my life around. This is my epitome. For the last twenty five years I've wasted my time, efforts and talent on getting drunk or stone or both. I shouldn't be here. I shouldn't be a janitor at a tribal casino either. I had dreams and ambitions of becoming a writer. Yet, I always came up short. I would give up so I could have a good time.

Right here and right now no more drinking or smoking. I can't afford this addiction anymore. It damn near killed me. This is my new life. I plan to make the most of it by being sober. I plan to make the most of by pursuing my life dreams and making it work, or at least die trying.

It's after seven and my parents are just leaving when my supervisor and two co-workers arrive. I'm sure it must be a shock to them. I'm never sick; I'm hung-over most of the time, but never sick. Roger is a grand-fatherly man in his sixties. He wears his bi-focal glasses like a badge of honor. He worked at Kaiser Steel for years, and then retired. Only to have my boss here at the casino hires him back because they were short-handed on supervisors. Despite his age he's still reasonably healthy looking and has no problem working twelve hour days. Elizabeth is the love of my life—at least secretly. She's somewhere in her early thirties, has long blonde hair that almost appears translucent, it's so fine. She has clear pale skin and a wonderful smile. She's tall and slender. She would be the perfect match for me, except she's married and has no plans to ever leave him. Bert is our maintenance guy who does great work when you can get him to work. He has a motivation problem. I don't know if he thinks this is some kind of government job and doesn't feel he has to put out effort to do anything. He's a nice enough guy; a bit overweight and arrogant. He tends to rub people the wrong way. I don't know if he means to, or it just happens. I'm surprise to see him actually. Elizabeth must need a ride.

I shake Roger's hand and say hay to Bert, while Elizabeth comes up to me and hugs me quickly. "What the hell are you doing here Jack?" Roger demands in false sincerity.

"I don't know. I thought just for shits and giggles, I'd pop a vessel in my brain."

"Well, I'll let you off today, but I'll expect you back by tomorrow morning bright and early."

"I'll see what I can do about that."

"What actually happened?" Elizabeth ask

"It's the damnest thing. I know I felt something pop in my head, and about ten, fifteen minutes later I about fall on my ass trying to get to the pool table."

"Well, I brought some insurance forms for your mother to fill out. We thought you were involved in some accident this morning. Then we got the call from your mother saying you had a stroke."

"Yeah, we couldn't believe it. You never get sick," Elizabeth agrees.

"Anyway our prayers are with you. Get better and that's an order," Roger says like a drill sergeant.

They all say goodbye and cut out the hospital room. I'm a bit surprised the ICU nurse allowed them in. Obviously they were given some type of time limit, like five minutes, before the nurse agreed to allow them in. Either that or they're claiming to be distantly related.

Tomorrow's a new day. Who knows what adventures await me.

I'm awake waiting to meet my physical therapist. I just had the pleasure of meeting the occupational therapist. It's Tim or Todd. Some name that starts with "t" anyway. He too is a harelip. I guess I pissed him off because I could see the moment he walked in the room that he had that curse, and I purposefully avoided eye contact so he wouldn't notice too. "Turn around," he commanded. I slowly moved my face to see his piercing blue eyes, his upturned nose, and the scar-tissue upper lip that defines who we are to everyone else. He's clean shaven and apparently displays his curse like a badge of honor. I can't do that. It's easier to hide behind a thick mustache than show the world something I'm ashamed of. He massaged my left arm and hand for ten minutes then left.

"Hello Jack, my name is Judy and I'll be your physical therapist," she states with beaming enthusiasm that quite impresses me.

Her accent is Japanese; she is definitely one that learned English as a second language. There's no mixing of "ls" and "rs" so she certainly had a good English instructor. She takes my right hand and gives it a firm hard grip that both surprises and impresses me.

"It's a pleasure," I reply. "You have a nice grip."

"Thank you. Now we begin." Like Todd before, she starts massaging my left leg. It seems to take forever before my leg begins to show the positive signs Judy is looking for. Then she raises my leg to a 90 degree angle to stretch my quad, groin and hamstring muscles. Considering, my leg probably weighs as much as she does, this action she does impresses the hell out of me.

"Now Jack, relax your lower leg, then try to raise and lower it, and then raise it back again." She commands this request between labored gasps as she struggles to keep my leg at a 90 degree angle. But try as I might, I can't even consciously relax my lower leg enough to do as she requests. She finally has no choice but to lower my leg back onto the bed. A thin line of sweat forms on her forehead as she states, "Jack, you have some serious tone issues."

I don't know if this is a good thing or a bad thing. "Isn't that good though?"

"Only in that you have strength and have the ability to walk again. If you have no tone, that means you have no muscles and can never walk again. I can do no more today I will see you tomorrow. Has Todd come in yet?"

Surely she saw him in passing. "Yes, he has," I reply in a tone that I'm sure belays the obvious. But either she didn't catch it or chose to ignore it.

"Good. Then I will see you tomorrow."

"Goodbye Judy."

I'm left alone with my thoughts now. Carol is right. I have been given a second chance at a new life. Not many people are given even that. I suppose it means, among others, not to revert back to my old habits of heavy drinking and cigarette smoking. But, I'm equally certain there's a whole mind set I must change to succeed. All the faults and flaws I committed these past years are behind me. The old Jack died last night on that pool table at the Moose Lodge. I must strive at making my self whole again, physically, mentally and emotionally. How I go about doing that, at this moment, I do not know. But as the old adage goes, every journey begins with but one step. And as Robert Frost wrote, "I have miles to go before I sleep, miles to go before I sleep."

I look at the window that shows growing shadows that signal the beginning of the end for this day, November 23<u>rd</u>, and soon night will take over. Right now, if I wasn't in this room I'd be collecting discarded cups and emptying butts from ashtrays into a can or paper cup. After work I would always drive to either the Moose Lodge or the Wagon Wheel to unwind. I would spend my Jackson or two Hamiltons and the rest of my cigarettes, buy a new pack before leaving the bar and heading home. Even though it's Friday night, I would have to force myself to leave so I can pull myself out of bed at five. Then the routine would start all over again. This routine is killing me. So what new routine will I start? No matter what it will eventually end up being a rut, like always.

I had ambitions of being a writer of novels and letters. When I went to college I was in the middle of a manuscript about a group of teenage kids, graduating from high school, being involved in a nuclear war, where only the hero survived with his high school sweetheart, who leaves him to become a nun. The end of the story he realizes he's been lied to all his life and must cope with other people's concept of right and wrong. I was ready to get an agent, when I made the mistake of getting my English professor/advisor to read and critique my work. He said it wasn't suitable for publication. I believed him and abandoned the project. Why the hell did I listen to him? He's just one person with his own faults and foibles. His opinion, while important, really shouldn't have held any more validity or weight than an editor of a publishing house or a literary agent.

So rather than be a published writer, I chose various jobs; the very reason I went college and avoid doing in the first place, and proceeded to become an accomplished drunk instead. I've never made more than twenty thousand a year. I've never own my own home, nor have a new car. Every endeavor I ever put myself in, I've had to work extra hard to strive at, or I just given up the effort altogether. I hate feeling sorry for myself. But, that's exactly what I'm doing. I get like this when I think what if . . . The reality of this is God placed me with the parents I have, the circumstances He or She put me in for one reason alone; to justify my existence on this planet and make the best of it. Then, by some miracle, try to change one small, minute aspect, and make a name for myself. Isn't that what life is really all about? It's damn frustrating, which I'm sure, is why I walked away from religion. I never really walked away from God though. I walked away from people that practiced to a god that isn't mine, and follow a set of morals I find fundamentally flawed.

They're just people after all, filled with attitudes derived from their own upbringing and environment. I hate this region I live in for this very reason. People here are fundamentally conservative; I'm liberal most of the time. People here tend to be more influenced by their morals and patriotism. I tend to want to be more influence by individual circumstances endeavoring to do the right thing. Too many people here tend to be narrow minded and bigoted. I'm more or less open minded. I moved to Seattle for one month in 1988. I loved it, but couldn't really get work, so made my way to Spokane for a couple months and ended up back in Tri-Cities where my parents lived. I should have tried harder to get work in Seattle. It fits me better socially, politically and spiritually.

My thoughts are suddenly interrupted when a middle aged woman in her fifties, curly brown hair, wearing bi-focal glasses and sporting a serious set frown that pronounced her facial wrinkles more, enters my room. Obviously she's another doctor that's come to prod and poke me or ask me more silly questions to test my cognition. "Hi, Jack. My name is DR. Charlotte Stannic, and I'll be in charge of your recovery."

"Well, you're the first doctor that's come in here to say they're actually in charge of my well being."

"Really? You've had other doctors in here?"

"It's been pretty much a revolving door of doctors parading in and strutting their stuff, then leaving. Is that even legal?"

It's the first time I've heard of it." I don't know whether to believe her or not. "It's certainly not very ethical." she replies. "Anyway, I looked over everything thus far and you are a prime candidate for inpatient recovery at St Luke's Rehabilitation."

"I never heard of it."

"Well, it used to be a hospital many years ago. A few years ago a group of doctors got together and bought the building with the intent of making a rehabilitating clinic. It's both inpatient and outpatient. We have specialists in stroke and pulmonary-care, as well as physical therapists and occupational therapists."

"So what will this do for me"?

"You'll be given the latest treatments and hopefully you'll improve enough to live a fulfilling and independent life."

"How much is this gonna cost?"

"Your insurance should cover 80 percent of it."

I'm not totally convinced, but okay. I guess it will be something that will help put me on the path to recovery. "I suppose I can give it a try. It's not like my calendar is full right at this moment."

"That's good." She gives me a pleasant and genuine smile. I get the impression my decision wasn't really an issue here. "The committee will decide within the next few days." With that being said, she shakes my hand and leaves. "I'll see you Monday. Judy and Todd will continue to work with you."

Maybe an hour later, I wake up and in walks my battery of bar buddies from the Wagon wheel. Two of the four are my golf buddies who I play with on Wednesdays during the summer months. The other two are women that I either shoot pool with or do Tuesday night darts tournament. Mary, is a computer programmer. She has black hair and brown eyes and recently divorced. Earlier this summer we watched movies at her place and I spent the night. She worried I had ulterior motives, but nothing happened. I don't know, maybe she wanted something to happened.

Judy is in her mid to late fifties and shoots a mean game of darts on Tuesday nights. It seems she usually wins or comes really close. I'm not sure what she does away from the Wagon Wheel. I just know her and her husband, Jack show up every night around five and am gone by around seven, except for Tuesday nights.

Rick works for a power company. I guess he's some sort of manager there. He has that certain charm that makes the ladies swoon over him, even though he's been married over twenty years.

Neal is a happy-go-lucky guy. He works as a maintenance guy for the local school district. He stands well over six feet and has solid muscles. Even though he's well into his fifties, no one in their right mind would mess with him. They're there to see me. I'm probably the most related person in Spokane. The guys shake my hand and the ladies give me hugs. "Cool, you look like Frankenstein," Mary announced with grin, as she ran a finger over my stapled scar.

"We expect you to be ready to golf with us by summer," Rick states with all sincerity.

"We couldn't believe our ears when your mother told us what happened yesterday," Neal told me.

"Yeah, we set up a fund for you to collect when you get out," Judy commented.

"Thanks guys," I said.

"Well, we better get going and let Jack rest," Neal suggested. I get more hugs and handshakes, then they're gone. I'm happy they care for me as me, rather than as another bar buddy. I hope they continue to feel that way further into the future when I'm sober for good. I have the feeling though I'll be just another historical footnote in the annals of the Wagon Wheel.

Eventually we all must die. When that day occurs or how, no one but the Great Creator knows. And what then? What will be my last thing I see? The last sound I hear? The last odor I smell? Or will I be a vegetable? Will death be sudden and overwhelming? Or will it be a slow painful disease that saps my strength and my will to live? It is for no one to know but our great Creator, by whatever name we place upon it, him or her.

All I know is the here and now. That, I can somehow control, to some extent. Right here and right now I am in control of my own thoughts, hopes and dreams. That is where my new life should begin.

Chapter Two

I t's Pearl Harbor Day and it's the day I leave this hospital to start my rehabilitation at St Luke's. While I enjoyed the hospital stay immensely, I'm equally happy to go to a different environment. Plus, Charlotte's enthusiasm over this rehabilitation thing, has got me pumped with added hope for the future. Whether its false hope is too early to say. But, this day is dragging me down with all this seemingly endless stream of red tape. I'm used to hurry up and wait; anybody who had to deal with military for any length of time knows once the initial phase of a mission is complete, it seems to take forever for the other shoe to drop to finish the task.

This is no different. Apparently, there are issues still to be resolved before I can be released. And apparently, these issues have nothing to do with me. I sit in my wheel chair. Not my wheelchair, I'm just borrowing it from this hospital. Nurse Carol has had to pull a few strings to get me a snack or something to drink while I wait. She comes over to check up on me. The room I occupied an hour ago is now cleaned and sanitized and ready for a new patient to occupy; I now occupy space in front of the nurses' station, my right hand clutching my medical records. My left arm is no longer a viable limb I can depend on for getting things done. It hangs suspended like a broken wing from some prehistoric bird. I hope that will change. Karen seems to assure me I will get use back. How much is very much an uncertainty.

While I wait here it's quite easy for my mind to roam and interpret the sights I see and my left side brain searches old memories and think back to pleasant times before the stroke. *I'm waiting in an office, no wait, it's a classroom at Eastmont Elementary School. I'm with mother. There's a lady there. Mother told me earlier I was to meet her because I'm going to school there and she's going to teach me how to talk better. "But, I already talk Mommy."*

"I know honey, but you can't talk for everyone else to understand."

"I understand me," I replied defiantly.

"I know dear. But, no one else understands you."

"I don't care about them. Why do I need to go to school anyway? Can't you just teach me?"

"I do, and always will. But I can only do so much and these people will teach the things I can't.

"Like what?"

"Oh, I don't know. Like Math for instance. I can teach you some of the things, but there's so much more about it I don't know or understand. These people know all of that."

"Mommy, who's that?" I point at pictures of two men. They're like the drawings I see her make from an easel with paint brushes. One man has white hair with a stern almost mean look. It doesn't look like the person that made the picture finished it. The other man has black hair and a beard. He wears a black string like tie and jacket. The other man didn't have a tie, just a white scarf.

"That man there is George Washington. He's the first President of the United States. And that man is Abraham Lincoln. He freed the slaves."

I looked at them and didn't think to highly of them; they're ordinary looking men. They didn't have halos like Jesus has in those pictures in Sunday School. We know what Jesus did was special because the Sunday School teacher tells us so. What else did they do?

This teacher walks in and introduces herself to me, "Hi there little boy, my name is Mrs. Blackburn. I'm a speech teacher and I hope to teach you to talk better." She turns to Mother. "I see he has a cleft pallet. Is he scheduled for more surgeries in the future?"

"Yes, but not for awhile."

"I see. I noticed you have the same condition. Is there anyone else in your family that has a cleft pallet?"

"No, he's the only child so far."

"No, I meant before you? In your genealogy."

"I think my mother's dad, my grandfather did," she replied in that way I later learn meant she had no idea, but threw it out there whether it was true or not.

"I see," she nods as she turns her attention back to me. "Now little boy. Tell me your name."

"Jack." I reply. Apparently though, I didn't pronounce it right.

"No. Not 'Gack'. You need to say it J A C K. Try it again, but slower so you can enunciate better."

I'm already bored with this lady with the bright red hair that's wrapped in that style Mother say is so popular because the First Lady wears it. I don't know who that is. "I know those men up there," I point proudly. "Geoge Wahington and Abrihan Lincin."

"You're losing focus. Pronounce your name."

"Mommy, can we go home?"

"Soon, tell the nice lady your name again, and we'll go home."

"J A C K." I pronounce impatiently.

She didn't like my attitude and slapped me hard across the face. "Do as your told little boy."

I stared back at her defiantly. "NO!" and I kicked her as hard as my four year old legs could kick against her shins.

"You little brat. How dare you kick me."

"How dare you slap him!" Mother responded angrily. "You don't touch my child. I'll have your job for that." She grabs my hand and drags me out the classroom. I went back to that school two years later, but never saw that speech teacher ever again.

A man carrying a clip board walks up to the nurses' station and asks for me. "Here I am," I reply.

"You got your medical records?"

I hand him the blue manila colored folder. He writes something on the clipboard then he wheels me down the hallway towards the elevator.

My ride has finally arrived to take me away from here. But wait, there's more. "I need to pick up someone else; a heart patient too," he announces. Great. Now I get to wait another thirty minutes. I might as well get back to my old room and spend another night.

Twenty two years earlier I'm at Reception at Fort Sill, Oklahoma. We are rushed out of our warm bunk beds at two in the morning, all sixty of us, lined in formation and marched to a building where our first appointment will begin. Obviously, they're not open. Nobody in their right mind is going to be open at this time of day. So we are standing at Parade-Rest for the better part of five hours before the building opens for the day. I could see, as my number was called, a sign on the door: Hours: 7AM to 4PM Monday thru Friday.

The bus driver wheels me down the hallway, to the elevator, to the lobby and outside to the waiting shuttle bus.

Then he disappears inside. I could see him through the side windows, adjusting seats, unlatching the back door and opening it. He comes back out with a remote unit that will lower the lift for the wheel chair and me to get up inside.

Once he has me inside, he straps my wheelchair using seatbelts that buckle securely. Then he leaves to pick up the other ride. I have no idea what to expect. I feel apprehension creep its ugly head again. Not as bad as when I was in Boy Scouts trying out in the swim test:

It's '73 and we're at Lake Wallowa, Oregon. There's a dock we have to take our swim test. I can swim, but I've never swam any distance before. I just jump into a pool at the local Elks lodge and swim, but not really. It's mostly splashing about and bullying the younger kids. Now, I'm being tested.

This is life and death, I feared. People were known to drown at this lake. The lifeguard is there to instruct us but mostly, he's there to rescue us from drowning. We're in line and each one of us get into the cold lake water. It's mid June and the afternoon sun is warm and pleasant. There's a slight breeze blowing in from the south. It's my turn and everyone in front of me passed the test. "I want you to get in, swim four laps, inside the roped area and float on your back for one minute," *the lifeguard instructs me. I jump in expecting the water to be as warm as the sunny day; it's not. I forced myself up to the surface to inhale air because the cold water has taken my breath away. I flounder helplessly. There's no bottom for my feet to grab to. I've forgotten how to swim and my worse fears are coming true. "Ah, Ah," is all that comes from my mouth. The lifeguard stretches the ten foot pole out and I grasp it firmly. He fishes me out from the lake.*

That's somewhat how I feel right now. I know this isn't life or death. But it is a nervous tension I'm feeling as the bus driver wheel an older man towards the lift.

We're underway as the bus driver moves the shuttle slowly out from the parking lot and onto Rowan Street. Spokane has all the big city congestion one would be familiar with at four in the afternoon. Tonight is no different. The biggest problem is this town has no north-south freeway to detour the congestion off the other north-south streets. There are plans in the works, since 1948, for a north-south freeway. But, according to conservative Republicans, the west side politician steal highway funds from Eastern Washington. I always see it from another perspective; that since there are twice as many people living there, it only seems logical the majority of highway funds go to the Westside.

We move southbound on Division until it meanders its way to Spokane Falls Boulevard, then Browne. We continue under the I-90 Viaduct, turn left onto Fifth then right on Chandler to the building that called St Luke's. It's dark and I'm not paying a lot of attention to the buildings outside appearance. It appears like it's a two story structure with large bay-like windows overlooking the grounds that in the spring and summer has maintained lawn and pine trees that provide abundant shade.

The bus pulls into the back entrance, where I assume, many years ago, had to be the emergency entrance. The reception area is there and people dressed in lab coats greet me. I hand them the packet. A plumpest woman in her forties sits behind a desk to retrieve it. She wears thick imitation tortoise-shell glasses and has a slight welcome to my world grin as she begins processing me into this facility. I look around at my environment; this place I'm to spend three weeks learning to use my legs and arm again. It's like any reception area one would come into. It's a small room with a very basic desk and comfortable chair, swivel back, I think. There's a computer monitor and keyboard the nice and pleasant lady uses to process my information. Her plump little fingers quickly strikes each key with expert-like precision.

"All done with that part of it Jack. Now we have to weigh you."

She's all smiles as I'm wheeled to a flat steel surface. An LED reads my weight plus the weight of the wheel chair. I'm taken off this loaner chair and placed on a St Luke's chair. She records the wheel chair weight and, I assume, subtracts that number to get a net total. My only question is, since wheel chairs are pretty much the same, should weigh the same, why can't they just have default or standard to go by? That way all they have to do is place whomever on the scale and be done with it. The computer would automatically calculate the person's weight.

I'm wheeled off the scale and a nurse takes me to an elevator. She presses the 1 button and we descend one level. She's pleasant to look at, except I just don't see that much of her because she's standing behind me the whole time. She tells me her name is Rachel. She's looks twenty something; fresh and youthful appearance; that radiant glow and lack of age lines gives her away. Her hair is blonde and shiny and clean. Her smile is bright and her teeth are straight and perfect. Her body is slender and long. She rushes me to the nearest nurses' station, where she leaves me to fend for myself.

Another nurse, her tag reads Carol, appears from the station and checks my records folder. She's probably twenty years older than Rachel and has experience written all over her face. But, that not saying she's unpleasant to look at. Her lines around her mouth and eyes show quite clearly. She's probably as slender as Rachel. Her smile is just as pleasant to look at. I'm sure her body is just as nice and soft to the touch as Rachel's. Carol looks tired, most likely from a busy work day. I don't know what her hours are here. Holy Family seem to work their nurses ten to twelve hour shifts. I wonder if it's the same here. Carol wheels me further down the hallway to room 121. There's an old man there with a younger woman and teenage girl. They're conversing in American sign language. The girl signs to him and he turns around to see me. He eyes me curiously, then his mouth broadens in a welcoming grin.

"George," Carol announces. "This is Jack. He's going to be your roommate." She tells him this loud enough to wake up the dead. I mouth "Hi George" to him. I know from my experiences with deaf people, it doesn't matter how loud you speak to them, they aren't going to hear you. Because of my own handicap, I have to exaggerate my mouthing, so they can understand me. Basically they rely on seeing an upper lip, which I lack, for them to understand certain words that one would expel. My sister learned sign language in high school when she was a teacher's aid. But I never did. I took French and remember little if anything from three years.

My sister, on the other hand, retained much of what she learned; going as far as working for the school district recently as a Teacher's Aide. She worked with three children in the kindergarten class at one of the schools there. I certainly wish she could be here now. He looks rather tall; maybe he holds his posture well. Because he's sitting in a wheel chair, it's hard to tell. I bet most men in this place are taller than me. I figure he's at least in his seventies. He has a full head of fine white hair, clean-shaven, wire-rimmed glasses perched neatly against the nose bridge. His nose is slightly hooked. I guess some people might describe it as regal or distinctive. His hands are active and his fingers positively fly about effortlessly as he communicates with his daughter and granddaughter.

"Dad wants to know your name," she asks

I point at myself and say "Jack."

"It's nice meeting you. I'm Jaclyn and this is my daughter Jill."

"Was he always deaf?"

"He became deaf in World War Two, when the bomber he was flying, exploded. Obviously it didn't destroy the plane, because he's still here. He thinks an oxygen bottle might have exploded when they were running through anti aircraft."

"So he was one of the lucky ones," I said to myself.

"What's that?"

"Oh, I'm sorry. Did I say that out loud?"

"It's okay. I'm sure his first wife thought the same thing. God has definitely looked over him all these many years. When he suffered his stroke, it was three days before his friend Mike showed to check on him."

Suddenly my attention to her is adverted when Mother and Dad show up. I even forgot Carol was still in the room. "Hey there, I see you made it."

"That damn rush hour traffic again." Mother replies. She runs her hand over the left side of my head and states, "you need a haircut."

"I'm sure I probably do."

"Hi there, how you doing."

"Mom he's deaf." I see he's still actively engaged in signing with his daughter and grand daughter. The daughter signs to him to turn around and greet Mother. He turns and waves hi to her back. I wonder if she relishes embarrassing me like that.

"I'm his mother and this is his dad too," she announces ten octaves higher than I feel she needs to.

Then, a man I never met before walks in. He has salt and pepper hair, neatly groomed and wired rimmed glasses. "Hi there, I'm Jim Calhoun and I'm here for Dr. Stannic. I'm glad to see you made it here okay." He shakes my hand, then my mom introduces him to Dad and her.

"What part of Texas are you from?" Mother asks.

"Oh some two horse town some thirty miles outside Austin."

Her smile broadens more. "Jack, I like him."

"Well, I'm already married ma'am."

Mother laughs heartily at this. I can't take her anywhere. "And you're a doctor too."

"Not quite ma'am. I'm Physician's Assistant, or PA. My parents could only afford to put me through the Masters program. But I'm still working on it though. Some day I'll be a doctor."

"Well, what do we owe this pleasure?"

"I just came in to make sure Jack here made in without a scratch."

"He needs a haircut."

"I see no reason why you can't give him one too. Also, I'm here to remove this catheter from him so he can go use the restroom again."

"About how long is he going to be here."

"It's pretty much to him. But usually, it takes about two to three weeks. Some people it takes longer, but that's really rare."

"Is he going to be able to drive again?" Dad asks him.

"Well, I can't see why not. Obviously he won't drive stick. He'll be having to drive automatic the rest of his life." He moves to the privacy curtain and closes us off from civilization. Dad and Mother excuse themselves from this momentous occasion, as the nurse comes in with a cloth covered tray. Jim dons the latex gloves as the tray is uncovered. A pair of vice-grip looking pliers lay there and Jim grabs these things and pops the catheter out from my penis. He hands the tube to the nurse, who disposes of it. She comes back and helps Jim to place me into the restroom, that's barely big enough for three people and a wheel chair.

Like a light switch, once I'm over the toilet, I begin to pee. Once done, I'm wheeled back to my bed where Mother and Dad are waiting patiently. Dad's trying to figure out the remote so that he can watch the news. "There's one more thing we have to do before we can let you go," Jim announces with glee. Just the tone in his voice made me wince in dread and apprehension. "You get the honor of using sonar gram to make sure your bladder is empty."

Jim and the nurse lift me from the wheelchair, so I can lay flat on the bed. The sweat pants are pulled down to just where my pubic hairline begins and the smear this cold gelatin over my stomach. The nurse runs this wand, which is also cold over my stomach. "It's empty Jack. You did well." He hands me a towel and I wipe off the slimy mess from my stomach. Well, duh. I could have told you that. I mean, really. Did they think I was going to purposely hold back my piss so they could take me back in there to force last remaining drops out of my bladder? I guess I'm not smart enough understand the logic behind that one.

"Jack, I need to get your father home. I'll be back tomorrow after work so I can cut that hair. At least then it will look evened out." With that they leave me here to fend for myself. I watch TV until I start falling asleep. I always have strange and vivid dreams, perhaps more so than most people I know. I always wondered about that; especially the déjà vu type dreams that comes back as reality in my conscious state. These dreams weird me out to no end. Then there are those dreams that I call reliving the past. This is one such dream.

I'm walking to my baby sitter's house after school. I'm quite happy. I'm mostly always happy because life is almost always good. It's 1969 and the sounds and smells of autumn are in the air. It's a warm Indian Summer day.

Just as I reach my baby sitter's house though, I witness a commotion of some sort from the baby sitter's neighbor. A man in his twenties, he's the older brother of a kid I know there, has a small dog dangling by its scruff, whimpering. I see it and want to scream at the man to stop, but nothing comes out. I watch the drama play out before my eleven year old eyes. The man goes to his pickup truck, grabs a claw hammer sitting in its bed and strikes the helpless puppy four times and throws the carcass in the bed like trash.

I awaken, and to this day, have never told anyone what I witnessed.

I don't know what would possess someone to do such harm to a helpless animal like that. One thing I do know, I looked at people a whole lot differently now. Or I should say, from that moment I witness this murder, I realized that no one can be innocent or trusting towards others again. And I wonder, could that have been the trigger that made me who I am today? Of course there are other incidents that occurred in my past that defined how I came to this point in my life. But, I have to say, this incident has continued to haunt me since. I know if he had seen me, or heard my screams, he may not had done what he did. But, then again, maybe it just didn't matter to him if there were witnesses to the crime. Something happened inside that house that made him so livid with rage he only could know of one remedy to make it right in his mind.

About the time I stop mulling over the past I notice a nurse or somebody walking into the room. My overhead light is turned on and the privacy curtain is pulled down the length of the bed. "Oh good, your awake. I need to draw blood from you." She's quite young, perhaps twenty one or so. She has a pretty smile and bright brown eyes. Her hair is brown like chestnut, and her face is without blemishes. She wears a smock that displays PAML. I'm assuming this is the company she works for. I would guess these people collect blood and read what's in them. I'm not sure where I fit in this, but she appears determined to collect my blood like a modern day vampire. She writes some things in her chart, wrapped my arm with rubber tubing, to expose a prominent vein, pulls out a vial, attaches it to a syringe looking needle, quickly inserts it into my flesh, and I watch fascinated as the blood rushes into the vial. She repeats this, then she walks over to my roommate and does the same thing. Then she comes back, turns out the light and leaves.

I know I just dozed off when the lights come on and in comes Carol scrambling into the room and getting me and my roommate up. She's nothing if not efficient. Like a drill sergeant mustering troops for PT formation, she does her level best to get the day started in the right direction. She works on getting George up and going. He seems a bit reluctant at first, then finally gives up the fight and gets dressed and groomed for the day's activities.

Then she comes over to me and starts getting me out of the gown and into a pair of sweats Mother left me to wear. She then wheels me to the dining area where men and women of all shapes and sizes sit in wheelchairs waiting for their breakfast. Most are given different types of pills they swallow down with juice. Then platters are laid out on orange or white plastic trays. Warming lids cover the plates. The tray is placed in front of me when I hear someone start choking on their meal. I wanted it to pass, but no, the old guy proceeded to spit out or throw up whatever was in his stomach or throat. That's not what I had in mind to a quiet dining experience. The nurses and a couple physical therapists help the poor guy get cleaned up. He's wheeled out of the room. I know I'll probably need help cutting the sausage I preordered the night before. Imagine my surprise when the cover lifted to reveal pureed sausage, like I had no teeth and needed to suck it through a straw.

Screw it; I'm not eating anything pureed or blended unless it's a milkshake. I ate the scrambled eggs, the muffin and the mixed fruit. "Carol, I'm done."

"You didn't eat your sausage."

"I don't do puree."

"Okay, then I'll have to inform Nancy." She says as she begins wheeling me back to my room. It's not more than five minutes later, Nancy, the supervisor, comes in. She's not heavy or slim, just somewhere in the middle. Apparently she doesn't like anyone making waves on her watch. She was in the dining area earlier dispensing medication to the patients. She has auburn hair she fixes in a tightly wound bun and wear wire rimmed glasses that kind of reminds me of one of those school teachers that ran those one room school houses.

"Why didn't you eat all your meal?"

"As I told Carol, I don't do puree. I assumed the diet selection I chose was the same as at Holy Family."

"No, it isn't. What you chose was a full liquid diet. And what you should have chosen was a general diet. Before we can give you that diet though, we'll have to monitor you to see if you can handle it."

So at lunch I'm placed to another room adjacent to the regular dining area, so they can watch me eat. Of course there are six others they are watching too. Short of having to feed them individually, these poor retches seem to choke on every other bite. It's almost as if the stroke they suffered affected their ability to swallow food.

Thankfully, I don't have that affliction, nor am I affected when I hear others choking on their food. I finished my meal, a whole wheat tuna fish sandwich and coleslaw. A few minutes later, the dietician comes in and helps me pick my meals for the next twenty four hours from the general diet choices.

The rest of the morning and afternoon is spent in three rooms, the dining area is utilized along with a main exercise room where all the mats and weights and elastic bands are kept. An office is also used. This is where the speech therapist resides. His name is Jack, and he wears many hats. He also monitors people's eating habits. And I guess he's also something of a social director. And he tends to work on those whose speech became affected.

I guess because I already have a speech impediment, he appears to take a special interest in me. I'm not sure why either. The first class I have is the occupational therapy and Ann is in charge of this. She is in her thirties, has weight issues, but is always in a good humor. I'm fitted with a peculiar hand brace that forces my hand to a flat state. Because my tone tightened my arm muscles, my hand muscle tightened too to where I have a fist all the time. This brace is suppose to straighten my palm out to its natural state. It's more cumbersome than helpful.

The first exercise she has us doing, us being six, is what she calls thumb circles. Here the palm is flat on the table and we rotate our thumbs in clockwise fashion. Then we are suppose to do it counter clockwise. I'm still trying to figure out how to get my thumb to do anything at all. It just sits there on the table, while I will it to move a micron so I know it's still a part of my body.

The second exercise is moving the wrists back and forth. I have to just manually move my left wrist with my right hand. I'm hoping the third exercise will involve something that is more to my ability. Not really though, this third exercise she wants us to raise our arms over our head and back from the table. I can only move it a few inches above my head before it starts to tone out on me and my arm turns into a broken wing. The final exercise she has us do are arm circles, where we rotate our arms in front of us clockwise, then counter clockwise.

I'm wheeled over to the gym next. Here is where the mats are, along various other hardware and weights and elastic bands of varying tension are used to strengthen limbs affected by the stroke. There are three physical therapists here conducting a myriad of conditioning and strengthening drills to increase coordination and stamina. There are several posters hung on the walls to inform and educate on what our limitations are, our pain gauge, and the like.

Pat is a twenty something brunette who seems to be in charge of the other two girls. She gets me from the wheelchair places me on a set of parallel bars. My left arm is really toned out, but she manages to loosen my muscles through a vigorous massage, so I can grasp my left hand to the bar. A piece of thin rubber material is placed on my hand so I can slide down the bar. I slowly take my first tentative steps towards other end. I basically am learning to walk all over again. I kick my left leg out, followed by my right. I repeat the process all the way down the thirty feet and back. My forehead is drenched in sweat. The whole ordeal takes five minutes to accomplish. Then I'm placed on the mat to perform vary simple and basic leg movements. I feel I'm making great strides today. This session seems to go by real fast. Then it's time to see Jack.

These sessions went on like this for the rest of the week. Then Saturday came. We worked half a day mostly because the physical therapists worked half a day. I think, for those people actually motivated enough, they're going to do exercises on their own. I opted to watch the Army/Navy football game instead.

The left hand stays flat at my side. And I wonder if this is my lot for the rest of my life.

Then, that evening, along with the usual preparations, the hand brace is also tied down and secured to my person.

"Carl, I don't think this will work out."

"What's the problem Jack?"

"This thing that you're attaching to my hand, how am I supposed to get any sleep with this thing on all night?"

"Well, Jack, here's the deal. Dr. Stannic wants that and we can't counter doctors' orders, now can we?"

"I suppose not. But, wouldn't it make more sense to have a well rested patient than a cranky one?" He appears to be gnawing on that tidbit. Than he responds, "Perhaps, Jack, but I don't want to jeopardize my livelihood over what your perceived wants are, compared to what the good Doctor has prescribed."

I can see this is a losing effort, with this guy. I finally acquiesce and allow the contraption to be tightened snugly over my hand and fingers. Even after I've finished taking my meds, I find it twice as difficult to relax enough to fall asleep. I'm sure I'll eventually get used to having this thing on me. Kind of like having shackles attached to your leg. I think most doctors are closet Sadists anyway. They go through their careers making their patient do or go through a variety of stuff that can only be described as archaic or barbaric. And then we pay them good money to do those things to us. So we're no better.

At least, the following day is Sunday. So what little sleep I had the night before, I seemingly make up for with little naps through out the day. But, the sleep I hope for, doesn't seem to materialize. Instead, I receive more visitors today.

Sergeant-Major January, with some officer that I don't recognize pop in and make their presence known. Today is drill day and our Christmas Party. Apparently, he feels obligated to come here to offer moral support for our detachment. Although our detachment has proven itself above and beyond our Westside based compatriots, we've been given little more than lip service; treated like red-headed step children. Why he's here in my room, I can only speculate. Sergeant-Major January was our company's First Sergeant, when he was promoted last March. I shake his strong right hand with a firm grip.

"Sergeant-Major, what a pleasant surprise." He's over six foot tall, which for an armor crewman, is quite tall and cumbersome. The ideal height is five foot nine and shorter. He has the military haircut that went back into fashion in the mid-eighties. His hair is black with some minor splotches of gray starting to form at his temple. He has a fairly large mustache that he constantly keeps trimmed. His body is quite lean, even for his age, which, I would assume, is credited to a fairly standard workout regimen. I can only guess that he's at least as old as I am.

"I'm just glad to see your still here, Jack. Is everything alright?"

"Everything is just fine. What brings you here?"

He gives me a quizzical expression and then replies, "We came up for the Christmas Party. And to see how you're doing."

"I'm doing quite well. I don't see me going back to the Guard any time soon. But I'd like to do what I can some day. If not, than it's been fun and quite a memorable experience." Then I move my eyes to the man that's been standing just behind the Sergeant-Major.

"Oh, I'm sorry Jack. This is the battalion X-O, Major Carlisle."

As officers go he doesn't quite come across as being real assertive or extroversive. He might be a little taller than me, with short brownish hair. He's definitely younger than me, maybe late thirties. And he's clean-shaven with a cleft chin and long thin nose. He's also athletic looking, with a slim runner's build. I shook his hand and his grip is slightly limp and sweaty.

"It's a pleasure Sir."

"The pleasure is as much mine as yours Sergeant. I heard nothing but good things from the Sergeant-Major and your platoon Sergeant and platoon Leader. I thought maybe I'd see a frickin halo over your head when we walked in."

"I turned that off this morning." We all laughed.

"Well Jack. I think we've taken enough of your time today." The Sergeant-Major states as he shakes my hand again.

"It's been a real pleasure," I reply. The X-O shakes my hand too and they both walk out the door.

Its maybe 30 minutes later I get another visitor, Mike Hunt arrives with his two sons. "Well, hey there Sergeant

Hunt. You just missed the Sergeant-Major and Major Carlisle."

"Yeah, I knew they were coming to see you."

"Didn't the First Sergeant make it?"

"I don't know what happened on that, Jack. He arrived yesterday for the PT run and the inspection, then he said, he had to go back to Gig Harbor. Anyway, the Sergeant-Major wants you to sign off on this waver. I'm pretty certain you still don't want to accept the promotion, like we discussed."

"That's correct. Are these the witnesses?"

"No, they're my two boys Jacob and Isaiah."

"Why doesn't that surprise me?"

"What's that?" He asks as he hands me the waver he needs me to sign."

"That you'd name your kids after people from the Bible."

"It's who I am."

"I know. I don't mean anything by it." I hand the signed paper back to him.

"Well, your all set then. I'll see you around, Jack." He shakes my hand and walks out the room with his two sons in tow.

About two hours later, Roger and Vicky arrive. His wife is actually quite attractive for her age, which I believe is somewhere between 55 and 65. She's slender and has few, if any, facial wrinkles. Roger introduces her to me and I shake her hand. "Here's the deal Jack. We had our present drawing for the employee Christmas exchange and I received your name. You don't need to get me anything, by the way." He hands me a gift box with a bow over the opening. The age of taking the time and effort to wrap a present, has long passed. Now its gift bags with the appropriate "Best Wishes" and "Happy Holidays" bannered across brightly colored bag.

I guess you really do have to look at life from both sides now, as Carol King stated in her song. I came into this place with an expectation that by some miracle I would walk out of this place like nothing happened. But strokes are funny creatures; you just can't expect miracles to take place unless you're willing to work real hard to achieve that goal.

I suppose a miracle did occur, that I had no idea would happen. When I read that guide to knowing and treating your stroke, it stated that, while drinking alcohol in moderation may be helpful, even healthy to some stroke victims, there are those that should never drink alcohol again. I read that and it was and is, to me, an epitome. A giant rock or brick fell from the sky. There it is, written in black and white, proof positive that I can't drink anymore; obviously its not rocket science, its common sense. I just never really practiced common sense when it came to drinking.

It's combination of many episodes in my life. There's the first time; I'm at John Jr and Cal's parent's place. They're twin brothers, whose dad always had a stock of Bud in the fridge located in the basement of their split level house. I didn't realized how nasty it tasted and asked myself, how can anyone drink this crap? I remember just drinking half its contents and threw the can into the Yakima River that conveniently flows below in front of their property. I felt more nauseated than buzzed as we went pheasant hunting the rest of the afternoon. There's the Homecoming Night where I'm just arriving home from a football game. I'm a high school senior and I had asked a lady friend to buy me some wine. She bought me a Chablis and a Rose. I chose the Chablis. It tasted surprisingly sweet. I only planned to take a couple pulls, then save the rest for later. But, I couldn't stop. Before I realized it, the fifth had been consumed. Mother and Dad were at the Moose Lodge, being Saturday night and all. I made my way to my room.

I remember feeling really good. I turned on some tunes, its back in the days of long playing record albums and I had inherited a hi-fi record player from Mother. I selected Steely Dan's Greatest hits, and maxed out the volume of that player. I sat on my bed feeling the music and the wine buzz envelope me like a warm blanket.

I didn't hear them come home. Mother came to my room, which in reality is a garage that I converted into a bedroom by throwing up a tarp against the door to somewhat keep out the cold, and placing my bed, a table I used as a desk, a dresser and my record player, that I placed on top of the chest freezer, next to the door. She shut the player off.

"What the hell's going on here?" She snapped angrily.

"I was playing some really cool music." I said. I don't remember if I was angry at her. I think I had become so drunk, that I thought it funny she would do that. She shook her head and closed the door. I don't remember anything after that. The next morning I wake just as dawn breaks into my room. I rolled over and felt something cool and sticky against my cheek. I placed my hand where this stickiness is. What the hell is this? Oh, shit it's my puke!

I'm fully awake now. I remember what happened up to the point of Mother shaking her head at me in genuine disappointment and closing the door. I somehow shut off the light and got naked and went to bed. Sometime during the night I got sick and puked twice, on either side of my pillow. I'm damn lucky, I didn't choke to death on my own vomit, like I hear so many people do.

The following year, I'm at Central Washington University in Ellensburg and I'm sitting in a dorm room down the hall from the room I reside in. I turned Twenty one and bought myself a pint of Jim Bean. I didn't have a glass to mix it, so I drank straight from the bottle. Before I'm aware, I finished the bottle and need to take a piss. But, when I get up and walk my way to the restroom, a more urgent need flows through my brain, and my stomach begins to churn like I've ingested poison. But, before I can release my stomach of its contents, my dorm brother informs me that there's a lady in the restroom, and that I have to wait my turn.

I'm ready to puke on him, but hold back, until the girl comes out. I rush in to the nearest toilet and release everything from my stomach. But, I'm not finished yet. I slowly fall to my knees and puke out black bile; then I dry heave. I can't seem to stop. Somebody comes in to check on me. I'm so sick, I can't even talk in any coherent way. All I can spout out is "bed." Two others help me up and drag me to my room. "Do you have your key?" Someone asked me. I can't talk out that it's in my pants pocket. It's an effort for me to nod yes. Someone else is digging in my pocket to pull out my dorm key. They get me on my bed. Sometime during the night, while they were checking on me, they found my head inside a trash can.

There was also the time, while I was going through my two year outpatient rehab. My boss, Jim was hosting his fiftieth birthday bash and barbeque. I drank more beer than I should have and there was a live band that played a familiar rock tune and I invited a girl to dance; I believe it was "Wooly Bully." When the song ended, the area we had danced was set next to a swimming pool, and I had in mind to toss her into the pool as a joke. Unfortunately, I'm the only one that thought it was funny. Her boyfriend didn't see any humor and proceeded to toss my drunken butt in to the pool anyway. Her brother, who arrived later, wanted to pick a fight with me. And the girl who I threw into the pool didn't think it was funny either.

I've been in trouble and I was lucky, I didn't get hurt or killed because of all the stupid things I did when I drank alcohol. But, mostly I spent money I didn't have and when it came time to buy something, or pay a bill, I didn't have money to spend. I ended up moving back to my parents because I didn't have a job and was going to be evicted from the apartment I lived in. I stayed sober for as long as it took before I found work. Then my evil ways would pop back into play.

Hopefully, I can stay sober for the rest of my life. I know it won't be easy. Nothing that takes effort and discipline ever is. So far, at least, it's been quite a bit easier because I'm in a controlled environment. The first time, I had to bend the environment. It only worked due because I made an effort to stay away from the bars and informed my roommate not to buy beer. But it didn't last. The first time I went back to the bars, I bought soda pop, until I met up with a drinking buddy who bought a pitcher of beer and had two glasses. That's all it ever took.

When I moved up to Suncrest, I stayed sober because I didn't have money to buy alcohol. One Saturday night though, I showed up at the Wagon Wheel, with money from a National Guard payment I received for the previous month. That night I met Peter who was playing Trivial Pursuit with just the question and answer cards. "You look smart," he started. "Want to play Trivial Pursuit?"

"Sure, but where's the gaming board?" I reply

"Our rules are a little different. *You get the answer right, we have to drink. You give the wrong answer, then you have to drink.*"

"*Sounds like fun.*"

"Which category do you want?"

"*History, I do best in history.*"

And so it went. He and Jo Ann, his wife and me played the Trivial Pursuit drinking game until the bar closed, and I was too drunk to walk home. They drove me home. I don't recall who was designated to drive.

I guess, now that it's all said and done with, it really doesn't matter.

Back to the here and now. It's dinner time again at St. Luke's. I sit down next Ken and Randy, and his wife Kim. Ken and Randy are near my age and their strokes came about quite unexpectedly too. They both appear reasonably healthy. Randy is a small business owner and Ken is a truck driver for a beer distributor. They both showed up three days ago after spending a week in a hospital. "So, are we having way too much fun tonight?" I ask as they wheel themselves at the same table I'm sitting.

"It's all pretty much the same thing. A whole lot of physical therapy." Ken states in a low key tone, as if he's bored with the routine already.

I catch this and state, "Ken, you still got at least four more weeks before they send you home. Don't get discouraged this soon into the game."

"I'm not used to this. I want to work with my hands; do something productive."

"Someone told me to be patient and it will all come together."

"I'm sure that person doesn't have a type A personality," Randy adds.

Our meals arrive and we begin to eat, when down the hall we hear this commotion, "Fucking sons of bitches, get the fuck out of my face you ass holes. We can also hear the nurse trying to calm the lady, who seems quite comfortable with her profanity laden vocabulary. "Honey, you mustn't talk like that in the dining room."

"You fucking bitch! I don't want to eat in your Goddamn dining room."

"Very well then, we'll eat in your room," the nurse calmly replies.

"That's got to be the love of my life," I state, hoping others in the room have the same sense of humor. Most of the men and some of the women laughed heartily. I'm fairly certain many of them were very much insulted by the exchanged conversation we couldn't help but overhear.

Nurse Nancy came into the room to apologize for what happened.

"Could I get her number? I want to take her to a church meeting or a press conference or the public library."

"Jack, you're beyond help. That poor thing has Tourette Syndrome."

"If that's what Tourette Syndrome is, than ninety percent of the people in the military and at most bars I've been to have that too."

"Unfortunately for them, they know what they're saying. She's not aware she is even saying that. It just comes out for some unknown reason."

"I'd still like to take her to a George Bush campaign rally. She would be quite entertaining."

It's the next morning and I'm dressed in my swim trunks and bathrobe. They want to try some aquatic exercises on me to see if my tone will minimize enough to do a productive workout. The instructor is Don, a forty something who's tall and muscular. Has wavy black hair that's starting to fade slightly to gray. Yesterday he happened into my room when I was just getting ready for my next physical therapy session. He started working my left shoulder, massaging it to the point of getting it totally relaxed.

"Now, I want you to stretch your arm out in front of you as far as you can. Pretend your reaching for something."

I did as he directed and struggled to reach out and as far as I could. It started out okay; got about three quarters stretched out before that tone kicked in again. Once that happened, my arm became mostly useless again.

"How are you around water?"

"I'm fine with that," I lied to him. The reality is, I tolerate water because I enjoy fishing more than anything. But, I wasn't going to admit that to him. Plus, I've started to get bored doing the same routine day in and out. I wasn't feeling like I'm progressing and need a change. *I still have flashbacks to my unhappy days in Boy Scouts struggling to swim even a lap. Private swim lessons didn't seem to help. I always felt it to be more a matter of stage fright; where in my desire to show I had to prove I could be like the other boys, I would overstep my boundary, freeze up and look silly as I floundered about in the lake water at Wallowa in North Eastern Oregon.*

I'm being wheeled to the pool area. It's surprisingly big. At least as big as a standard size Olympic pool. I think this is most likely a recent addition to this place. I couldn't imagine any regular hospital having a swimming pool set up in the basement. There's also a hoist to raise and lower patients in and out of the pool. I'm feeling the same anxiety as I felt in my unhappy days in Boy Scouts. I suppress it though, replacing the negative with positive. After all, I know where my limits are now and the last thing Don is going to have happen is me getting hurt.

Another Girl or lady is in the pool, and her instructor is preparing to hoist her out. Dan grabs the hoist controls, moves the crane back over the pool and lowers the cradle to the water's surface. The instructor then sets the paraplegic lady/girl on the cradle and straps her in. Dan, once the instructor gives him the hand signal to raise the hoist, pushes the up button on the remote control. The cradle lifts up and, when it's at the desired height, Dan moves the crane over to where the empty wheel chair sits. He lowers the cradle to perhaps a quarter inch from the wheelchair's seat. Then her physical therapist, which has already pulled her lithe and muscular body from the pool, unstraps the lady/girl from the cradle. The gravity pulls the weight of her body effortlessly on to the wheelchair.

"Okay Jack, it's your turn." Her physical therapist then moves the girl/lady a safe distance from the pool, and helps Dan get me strapped in. Her blondest hair wisps peek out her bathing cap. I never cared for those for some reason. It tended to push everything down, making the wearer's face look pinched and ugly. "Thanks for your help Sue," Dan tells her grapefruit shaped breasts.

"Your welcome," Sue replies, not realizing where his eyes are directed, or perhaps she has grown accustomed to men's leering eyes. "If you want to get into the pool, I'll let him down to you and I can put everything up."

"That works for me," he replies. He pulls off his sweat pants and sweat shirt, exposing formidable pectoral, bisects, trisects and scapulas.

He wears a tight fitting bikini type suit that enhances his abdominal muscles, buttocks, quads and hamstring muscles. I notice both females are enjoying the show, especially when he turns his back to them and dives into the pool like a professional swimmer. I would had preferred he'd ask her to be in the pool unstrapping me. She expertly moves the controls, lifting me up, swinging me over the pool, and lowering into the water. It's quite warm, just slightly cooler than bath water. My apprehension is fading fast and I feel more self confident. Before he releases me though, he straps on a brace to my left leg. He must have rummaged through the toy drawer picked out the first brace in the pile because it didn't fit right at all. It felt as if it should have been made for that paraplegic girl/lady sitting in the wheel chair, who is now leaving with the hottie physical therapist. "This seems a bit small," I tell him.

But he seems to ignore my criticism and unstrapped me from the cradle. This side is reasonably shallow; perhaps it's four or five feet. I can plant my right foot down quite easily. But, my left foot is tending to kick out a bit. He moves over to the three foot area. The brace is quite uncomfortable now. What was he thinking? There's a brace sitting in my room that fits me just fine. "How's that brace feel?"

Now he asks me. "It feels really tight and small."

"Sorry about that. It's the only one available. We'll get through this and then tomorrow I'll try and find a bigger brace for you to wear. Try and stretch your leg out a bit. Then try and bend your leg."

I do as he instructs, but I think the fact that this brace is pinching my leg, is affecting the desired result he's looking for from me. After a bit I'm able to do as he directed, but it's painful and uncomfortable.

"Now, let's try to walk on it." Right, not right now, it's going to happen. I plant my left foot onto the brace and the pain is that much more intense. But, after a bit of coaxing on his part, I take my first actual steps sans the support of a walker or cane. "Good job Jack. You re well on your way to walking on your own again."

He's has me resting against the side of the pool. It feels like this brace is cutting off my circulation. "That would be great. I wish though, that I could get the same results from my arm. I would have thought, since the arm is closer to the brain that the arm would recover before the leg."

"Nope, and I'll tell you why. There are three times more muscles and nerves in the arm than in the leg. It's a lot easier to get your leg back first, than the arm. Have faith it will come."

That seems to be the mantra here. Faith, or a belief that hard work, perseverance and a positive attitude will guarantee a desired outcome. It probably isn't that simple. There are just too many variables in life to make that happen. After all, that Murphy guy is a real asshole. If anything can go wrong, it will. If you want something to happen, a pinch of good luck seems to trump hard work and perseverance every day. That's been my experience in this life I've lived so far. Of course I'll work hard for everything I want. Most of the time I might get it too. But, it's the luck factor, that I seem to lack, that prevents me from attaining the golden egg.

We never did the water therapy again. I don't know why, except he probably sensed my apprehension to water. Or, he couldn't find a big enough brace for me to fit into. Or, any number of other excuses that popped up, making it impossible to work out. It's not that important. I like to call it a mind over matter dynamic; I don't mind and it doesn't matter.

It's getting closer to Christmas. George has been given his walking papers. His daughter has packed his personal belongings into an overnight bag, and she's going to drive him to a nursing home where he'll most likely die from boredom. I shake his hand and wish him luck in his short future. I watch Carol wheel him out the room and down the hallway to his daughter's waiting car.

These places are now called retirement villas or gardens; anything but nursing homes. Years into the future I will get my first taste of one of these nursing homes when Mother and I have to place Father for a period of time. There's nothing pleasant or serene about the experience I came away from. I certainly don't want to end my final days on this planet slowly wasting away like a rotting fruit on a vine. But, that appears to be the situation for a lot of these people. It almost seems more humane to do as the Eskimo people do with the old ones; place them on a Kayak and push them out to sea without a paddle. What we seem to do with our elderly is no less barbaric.

Back to the here and now, so to speak. I mentioned it's closer to Christmas, and one of the physical therapist, I think her name is Brenda, a very pretty twenty something, asks me if I'd like to check out the Christmas light displays around certain neighborhoods in Spokane. I've been itching to do something different here; this would be the ticket. Father and Mother always took my sisters and me on these nightly adventures and we enjoyed it immensely. "Sure, that sounds like fun."

That evening, just after dinner, I struggle to get my coat on over my left arm. For some reason, I can't figure, my tone has suddenly reared it's ugly head and I can't relax my left arm to push into the coat sleeve. It's completely stiff and useless. "Tell you what Jack," Brenda suggests. "Let's just wrap the coat over your shoulders."

"Sure, whatever works. Far be it for me to hold up progress."

She wraps the coat like a shawl and wheels me out to a waiting shuttle bus. I'm hoisted up on the lift and am strapped in. Two other wheel chair bound patients and one, Dorothy, who walked on the bus without assistance. Her stroke only affected her speech; in that she's as mute as George is deaf. Not a word passes through her lips. Other than that she does the other exercises quite well, to the point where she really doesn't need to bother being here in an inpatient class.

Along with Brenda, one other therapist has volunteered her time to enjoy the ride. She's a pretty blonde named

Candy. We're all bundled up and ready to step out and away from the rehabilitation facility for awhile.

"Okay, everyone, let's sing some Christmas carols to get us in the Christmas Spirit," Candy suggests with the enthusiasm of a high school cheerleader. "Jingo Bells, Jingo Bells, laughing all the way. What fun it is to ride in a one horse open sleigh." That's as far as it went, when she realizes she is the only one singing, and the bus pulls out of the long driveway and onto Spokane Street and down to Fifth. It appears we're heading north first, which surprises me because I would think most Christmas displays are on the South Hill, where the big money is. Unless, of course they're heading up pass Garland area. Then it gets more into middle class where people can afford to put out Christmas displays.

So we continue north to just around Glass, where we're up above the poorer working class neighborhoods that lack such displays. Once we arrive here, there are a number of brightly lit displays that show a myriad of colors and designs. Each house is unique and creative in their approach to interpreting Christmas. Some just show brightly colored Christmas lights, others utilize the more uniquely Christian displays, such as the Nativity. Still others have Santa, elves and reindeer on display. I soak it all in to my still working brain. The creative portion that likes these kinds of things. I'm sure if my left brain hemisphere had been affected, I most likely wouldn't had even been interested in going.

Since my creative juices flow from my left brain, I'm more inclined to enjoy stuff like this field trip we're taking. Maybe that's why no one else is talking too much about it. The one person that is talking about it is Helen.

I met with her about a week ago when Tom had us together. On this occasion he wanted to see if we knew how to write out a personal check. More likely he wanted to gauge if we remember how to write out a personal check. I did; and I had mine written out in about two minutes. I was still struggling with the ability to write anything right handed and eights seem to be my nemesis. Helen, on the other hand, apparently never learned to write checks in her entire adult life. She's a bit bovine in appearance and manner. I have no idea what her stroke took it's toll on, but it appears, before the stroke, her husband did pretty much everything for her.

"I never wrote checks," She complained to Tom.

"Well then, Jack's done writing out his check and I'm sure he won't mind walking you through it," Tom replied not hiding his displeasure towards the forty something woman with the annoying whiny voice.

Reluctantly, I pick up a pen to patiently explain the how to of writing out a check; something I learn to do when I was growing up. "Okay, The first thing I do is write out the date of the check up here, where it says date. Then I go to the line that says make out to the order of, and write out the person or company's name. Then I put in the amount here in this box. I then write the amount out on this line here . . ."

"Why is that?" She asks in that annoying whine of her hers.

"Because, if you write out the numerals, let's say ten dollars, and leave that portion blank, then that person can make it out for ten thousand dollars and you'd have to honor it, even though it's fraud and forgery. Now you write out the amount exactly as the amount you ledger on the box up here. Where there's a cents, you put the cent in as a fraction of the total amount, say 10/100 for ten cents. Then you write what's the check is for, say groceries, and finally you sign it."

"Very good Jack. Now Helen go ahead and do as he showed you."

Now we're listening to her complain in that annoying whiny tone of hers. "It's so cold back here." "I can't see the lights very well." "Oh, they're so pretty. I hope my husband has put out the lights too." And on and on she goes. I think we all breathed a sigh of relief when they parked the shuttle at the main entrance and we all disembarked from the bus. I know I did.

This morning Cathy wants to see me dress myself. I'm not sure what that would accomplish. After all, until recently, I've dressed myself without help since I was two. But, I'm nothing if not accommodating. She watches me as I remove my underwear and t-shirt to put on clean. Taking off is always easier than putting on for some reason. I certainly can't explain why I'm having this much trouble putting on my underwear and t-shirt. It's not going on at all. The more I attempt to put my t-shirt over my head and move my right arm in the sleeve, my left arm stiffens to the point that I can't get it into the left sleeve. The more I try, the more maddingly frustrated I become. I give up on the t-shirt and do the underwear. Maybe that will be easier. So I put the left foot out to the area the left leg is suppose to go and set my right foot next to it. I bend to raise my drawers up to my butt like I've always done. It won't work though. Why won't it work? It always worked that way before. Now though, nothing wants to cooperate.

"Is there anything I can do to help?"

It's her fault. How dare her; humiliate me like this. I'm totally pissed off now and she wants to offer assistance. "Not now! I think you've done enough already." She leaves the room. Good riddance, Goddamn Bitch! Screw it all, I'll just stay in bed today and feel sorry for myself.

Carol comes in. "Jack, what's the matter?"

"Nothing! I'll just stay in bed all day."

"You're not going to do that. Let me show you how to dress yourself."

"Fine, like I've never dressed myself."

"Well, no Jack; not since your stroke. Remember you don't have two independent arms and legs. You have to adjust and accommodate accordingly. You always start with your weak side first. Eventually, you'll be able to able to use your weak side to help the right by holding on to an article of clothing. So, place the left sleeve of your t-shirt over your left hand and then place the right sleeve through your right arm and pull the shirt over your head. That's it Jack. Now your underwear and pants are a little bit more complicated, but not after a bit of time. Just cross your left leg over your right, that's it. Now, place your underwear though the left leg, uncross your left leg and now put your right foot through the right opening, and now you can pull up. Do the same thing with your pants now. Good, I think you got it Jack. Your socks are the same way, weak side first and the your shoes. I'll help you tie them. Okay, last is your sweat shirt. Left arm will go first, followed by right and pull over your head. Your done Jack. Outstanding job."

She leaves the room to go help another patient and I'm left here wondering what purpose Cathy was trying to prove, except what a lousy instructor she was. Rather than provide me with guidance and a method to succeed, instead she did nothing but set me up for failure. Then, when she did offer, I lashed out at her in my anger, she leaves the room to get someone else in that can better handle the situation.

A few days later Cathy is working with me again. I don't know, maybe she's a glutton for punishment. "Jack, today we'll show you how to get in and out of a tub by your self." This ought to be interesting.

"To start with, I'll help you out from the wheelchair, and help you sit on the tub's edge." She wheels me near the tub and proceeds to help me from the wheelchair and onto the tub's edge. It's a large tub; larger than the one at my parent's house. The bathroom is larger here too. There's no way this wheel chair would fit this far into the bathroom. There's grab bars strategically set up on the tub's side, either vertically, obliquely, or horizontally to best accommodate the person's needs.

"Okay, now that we have you on the tub's edge, scoot your but over a bit. I mean turn it so your kind of at an angle. That's it. Okay, now place your strong arm over to that grab bar, put your right foot inside the tub and slide yourself into the tub." I do as she instructs, but I don't think this is very safe. It doesn't feel like I would have much control, and I might get hurt. She notices that too after do this.

"Okay, I messed up. Wait here a moment." She leaves me a moment and brings in Carol. "Yeah, I think I got it backwards or something."

"You did Cathy. To get into the tub, have him grab the safety bar first, then he can use his strong side to put him into the tub, like that Jack, real good. Once he's in the tub, he can set himself down. That's a good job Jack. Now to get out, use the safety bar to pull yourself out of the tub, that's it, now place your butt on the tub's edge, turn your left leg until it's right against the tub's edge then move the leg up and it should plop on the ground. Finally you can raise yourself up and back into the wheelchair or whatever. Eventually, Jack, you won't have need of any walking devices."

"I can't wait."

Another day and a new thing to do that will get us back to more meaningful independent life. On this day, a group of us are heading to another room away from the familiar dining room we've grown accustomed to. This room is set up like a one room apartment. It has all the accommodations one would find in any apartment in Spokane. Most important for today's situation, is a kitchen with range and refrigerator that has food stuff that we all requested to make our own breakfast. I proceed to start prepping for scramble eggs, sausage patty and toast. It used to take me about fifteen minutes after all is prepped and cooked before I consumed my breakfast. A lot of times I would be real adventuresome and make sausage gravy and biscuits, mixing the concoction together into what the military would term S.O.S.

So I start the process. I find a skillet to heat up on the stove top. I never forgot how to cook, it's just the first time I've had to do everything one handed. Having never cooked on this stove before, I'm not familiar with the range's idiosyncrasies such as its heat setting. I set it on mid heat, and realized the setting is too high for what I want to do. I should have put the toast on first. I threw the sausage on the skillet and it immediately starts frying and popping hot grease everywhere. I immediately lower setting to low heat, but the damage is done. Now I'm pressured to put out a good meal without being properly prepared.

I'm rushing to throw in the toast to get it ready and frantically flipping the sausage patty to keep it from burning on one side. I'm still waiting on the eggs because I don't want it to burn before the sausage is ready. But now is another problem. The sausage is cooking too slow and I'm under additional pressure because Michelle has put a thirty minute time limit. The toast is done and I put butter on it, one handed and realize what challenge this is. The toast won't stay still for me at all. In the meantime, the sausage needs to be flipped again. I should have crumbled the sausage into bits rather than make a patty. I would have been done. I flip the sausage one last time and break two eggs and the have the desired affect when they plop onto the skillet already broken. I mix it quickly. I shut off the heat. I mix the eggs a little more, than I pull the skillet off the stove top. Michelle took the liberty to place my toast on a plate and set the plate in close proximity to where I'm working. I throw the sausage and scrambled eggs onto the plate. It's almost perfect' the eggs are slightly undercooked and the sausage is a bit over cooked. The toast is cold now. But it all tastes good with the knowledge I accomplished this feat myself.

Today I'm finally leaving this place that I've grown to love and loathe. This St. Luke's Rehab that has taught me to function in a semi-paraplegic society, this place where feeling sorry for yourself is frowned upon and feeling good about yourself is encouraged.

I have mixed feelings about this place because I'm still confined to a wheelchair and my left arm is as useless as tits on a boar. But, I have a much better attitude towards life and living than I did before my stroke took have my body and brain away. Now I must work at getting those back.

Today I'm given my walking papers. There's nothing more for these fine folks can do for me. It's on to home and a group of physical therapists will work with me there. I feel ready too. Let someone else have this room so they can recover and go home. Mom is here, and so is Bessie, a family friend I've known since I was eight or nine. She's quite short and used to be very feisty. Today, she has a gray streak flowing down her brunette hair. She hugs me with the same familiarity of a family member. I'm not sure why she's here though. "What brings you here Bessie?"

"Well, it's a long story," she starts with her signature Boston accent she brought with her when she met her ex-husband over forty years ago. "I was coming to see my grandsons, and my car broke down. I thought, since I'm here I'd call Mary and Warren and see how everyone was doing. I never thought you'd be here recovering from a stroke. But I'm glad to hear you're going home today."

"Well, your not the only one," I reply. I have my hand in that brace and Mom has brought the Jeep Cherokee to load the wheelchair and walker.

"I don't know why you're taking all this stuff too. There's no room in our house for that." Mother complains to me, like I had anything to do with the decision.

"I don't want to, but they seem to think I need to, at least for the time being until I can start doing things on my own."

Getting out of here is actually more seamless and painless than the fiasco at Holy Family Hospital. By noon, we are checked out and wheeled to the Cherokee, where I make my first attempt at getting into her SUV, that's a much higher platform than the '88 Crown Victoria I had practiced on before.

We're in and heading to the pharmacy at Rockwood Clinic that's located on Fifth and Chandler. Bessie and I are alone in the car and she informs me that John is waiting on her at an apartment in Browne's' Addition. "So, Jack what do you think caused this?"

"I think my bad habits caused it."

"Well, that's understandable. We all have bad habits that tend to get us in trouble for one reason or another. What are you going to do now with your life?"

I know what I want to do; go back to living a normal life again. I just don't know how that will happen just yet. "Get better so I can go back to work."

Mother arrives with my medication. I have no idea what it is or what it's suppose to do for me. I wish they'd legalize marijuana, then there wouldn't be this hassle we have to deal with. Bessie gets hold of John her cell phone and informs him we're on our way to where he's at.

Browne's' Addition is located across downtown. It's extremely historic consisting of Victorian and Georgian style mansions built at the turn of the last century. There are also a number of apartments that apparently came afterwards. John sits outside one such apartment, smoking corn cob pipe. He looks like a wild mountain man with hair just below his ears and sporting a fairly shaggy beard, that's reddish gray, like the hair on his head. He sports a ball cap with a Jack Daniel logo emblazoned on the brim. I roll down the side window and, with a degree of emotion I don't expect, say "hey brother. How you doing?"

"I'm good," he replies grasping my right hand in firm grip. He wears glasses that hide his eyes to the daylight. It's overcast. "I understand you just got released from a rehab."

"Yeah, I had a stroke, but hey, I'll be back on my feet soon."

"Good, I'm glad to hear it. Take care and I'll get in touch with you soon."

"See you John." He helps his mother out from the Cherokee and closes the door, his six foot something frame towering over his mother's five foot frame. I watch them disappear into the apartment.

We go to Northern Quest Casino in Airway Heights, where I work.

They're in the middle of a major expansion on their South half. This is the first of many such expansions they'll perform in the years to come. It's painted in a typical native motif of southwestern desert browns, tans and turquoise on a box shaped building. The greenery consists mostly of sapling and yearling firs and pines, with some shrubbery mixed in.

Mother parks the Jeep near the North entrance, pulls out the wheelchair from the back and wheels it toward my door. She helps me out as best she could and I sit down in the wheelchair as Michelle and Carol directed me. Mother then wheels me into the building amid the smoke and noise of several hundred slot machines making a myriad of whistle and bell and buzzer like sounds to attract the gambler in all of us. If one can't hear, there's always the flashing lights to attract the gambler, like a moth.

I'm right at the employee entrance when one of my housekeeper co-workers happens to come out. It's not Elizabeth but Lena, a native girl who is Amazon like, with high cheek bones and bright, pleasant smile. She gave me a quick hug, then told Mother, "I'll take this from here," and proceeded to roll me in through the employees' only double doors. I'm wheeled through the back hallway to where the housekeepers tend to congregate when not on the gaming floor, the Supply Room. This is the original supply room that is set up as a place to store all the casino's cleaning, paper and liner products, but also is the maintenance area where their tools, paints and other vital equipment is stored. As the casino continues to expand, efforts will continue to be made to move the supply room to various locations throughout the back of house area. It's almost as if the powers upstairs are more interested in finding office space for managers than in keeping facilities department happy.

But, that's for another chapter. At this very moment Elizabeth and Roger, with Kane, a native Blackfoot from Montana with big, broad frame and equally broad smile, and Igor, a transplant from Croatia, who's as big as Kane. I think they just happen to all be there because most of the time, they would be out on the floor. They're wearing the latest in Housekeeping apparel, a burgundy button down shirt that looks good on the men but, looks like a tent on Elizabeth and Lena. Roger is dressed in a Maintenance shirt with Northern Quest Casino emblazoned on the left breast pocket. He walks over to me and grabs my right hand, giving it good firm squeeze. His handshake is genuine, like the person himself. He tells it like it is. "It's good to see you finally made it back. You're looking good Jack. Well, as soon as Dan comes in we can give some early Christmas gifts from us and the casino."

"I see the South expansion is coming along quite nicely. When are they planning on getting done?"

"Oh, I don't know, possibly in a couple months, barring anything unforeseen."

About this time Dan comes through the doorway. He's about six foot six or seven, and is always checking high areas for dust. Areas no other person would imagine checking. His argument is a customer doesn't need to be in contact with any dirt no matter where. "Jack it's good to see you back. This is your yearly bonus check, this is notification of your annual merit increase, and this is a check from your team members to help pay the medical bills that we all know are going to be there. I'm just happy see you alive and getting better." He shakes my hand with a firm grip.

"Thanks Dan. Thanks you guys, and everyone else from the casino. I guess I need to make out a thank you card for the casino."

"We think you deserve it," Elizabeth responded with emotion affecting her voice.

"Do you want to take an impromptu tour?" Roger asks.

"Sure, I suppose that would be okay."

"Good enough, then. Lena, go ahead and show him the new section and meet his mother wherever she is."

"I'll be happy to," she replied. She wheels me out the Supply Room, down the hall, and to the security area, where she hands me a plastic construction hat, and then we enter the new South expansion area. She wheels me down a still uncompleted hallway where tin posts that will eventually serve as studs, stick up vertically, waiting for particle board to be hung. She shows me a fairly large room where the Pend Oreille Pavilion will be located. The pavilion presently has been a large nylon tent with portable, folding chairs. "They say, they'll have Vegas-like acts come here to perform. I say, 'we'll see.' Apparently, though, this is going to be temporary, until they do the north expansion."

"When will that be?"

"A year or two."

"Why don't they just wait until they do the north expansion to do this pavilion thing?"

"I know. None of the Elders have any common sense. I think they're listening to the wrong people."

We continue into a larger room still; about a third again larger. "This," she explains, "will be the new South gaming floor." It will definitely add to the gaming experience when it's done. It definitely will add twice the floor capacity as the present site. Besides the description Lena gives me on what will be, it is still just a barren large room. The real action is on the other side of the plywood walls where slot machine sounds can be heard. She opens a plywood door, and she wheels me back to the here and now.

We find Mother in the lounge drinking a soda pop and munching on some nuts that are sitting in decorative crystal jars centered on a table she's sitting. "How are you doing?" I ask as I'm wheeled to her table.

"Rotten. I put twenty in and went bust in about five minutes."

"That was pretty fast. Now you know why they're called one arm bandits."

"I'll say. Well, let me finish this drink here, and we can head to your next stop."

"Which stop is that?"

"Your Wagon Wheel Tavern."

"Oh, okay I can do that." She finishes within five minutes and we're back on the road heading towards Suncrest. It's exactly twenty five miles from my parents' place to the casino. I never thought I would be commuting this kind of distance, but in Spokane, it seems normal to commute such distances. I would just assume move closer to work to save wear and tear on the car and money on fuel. I guess though, most people here are more interested in living in bedroom communities, then driving long distances to work miles away than in saving time and money finding work close to home.

After forty minutes, we're driving into the town limits of Suncrest. It's the second largest town in Stevens County, and it's unincorporated. It consists of very expensive homes, on streets without sidewalks. The whole business district is a pair of strip malls with a grocery, hardware store, beauty salon, pizza restaurant, another café, a dentist, a psychiatrist, and some marketing store, a party store that specializes in party rentals, balloons and favors, and a video store. In between the strip malls are a gas station and The Wagon Wheel. It's motif is rustic, western with the unfinished boards and unpainted doorway. There's a bar on the left, round tables and western style chairs in front, along with two buddy bars that are set just in front of the main bar. Up the room are two pool tables that sit on a laminate dance floor. On the south wall are electronic dart boards that are used every Tuesday night for dart tournament. An actual separate room for family dining is in the south portion of the building.

Tonight, it's Christmas Eve and the place is only open for another half hour, before they shut down for the night. As is traditional, the owner has allowed people to bring dishes of finger food in to mark the occasion. She mixes up a batch of special recipe eggnog and hot buttered rums. The place is filled to capacity. Many of my friends are here, shaking my hand or squeezing my shoulder, or in the case of several women, lots of hugs and kisses.

Tara, a sweet blonde that is tall and slender with mischievous smile, starts to grab a beer mug, "The usual Jack?"

"No, I'm afraid not. I'll have a root beer tonight."

"Oh, well, okay then," she responded with mock disappointment.

She pours out a mug of Henry Weinhardt Root Beer and hands it down to me, and gives me a quick hug and kiss. "I want to thank everyone for the well wishes and prayers. It's really helped me a lot," I yell out to everyone over the din. Tara then reaches in the cuss jar and hands me an envelope. I open it and find more cash than I can remember seeing in one envelope. "Well, Merry Christmas to me," I exclaim with more than a little emotion. "Thanks everyone."

Finally, Mary wheels me out to my Cherokee. She helps me out from the wheel chair, and while Mother places the wheel chair into the back of her rig, Mary gives me a quick hug and kiss. I return the kiss, first to her cheek, then on her lips. Then she leaves, while Mother helps into the SUV. "What was that all about?" Mother asks.

"She was just wishing me a merry Christmas."

We are home now. I'm not a religious man, and made that point quite clear when chaplains would drop by. It's not that I don't believe in a Christian god, I do. I just am completely turned away from religion, especially the kind as preached by the likes of Jack Falwell and Pat Robertson. Their god, is a righteous, ill-tempered god who thinks we deserved 9/11 because we're a godless society. My god, on the other hand, is a kinder, gentler god that is forgiving, that carries you when you need to be carried. Falwell and Robertson's god is full of fire and brimstone and is more interested in judging and persecuting real and perceived wickedness. My god is charitable, feeds the hungry and offers hope for the desperate. Their god, according to them, is a Republican. My god, on the other hand, has no political agenda or beliefs.

On occasion I do read the Bible. One of my favorites is in Luke Chapter Two:

> And there were in the same country shepherds abiding in the field, keeping watch over their flock by night.
>
> **9**And, lo, the angel of the Lord came upon them, and the glory of the Lord shone round about them: and they were sore afraid. **10**And the angel said unto them, Fear not: for, behold, I bring you good tidings of great joy, which shall be to all people. **11**For unto you is born this day in the city of David a Savior, which is Christ the Lord. **12**And this *shall*

be a sign unto you; Ye shall find the babe wrapped in swaddling clothes, lying in a manger. **13**And suddenly there was with the angel a multitude of the heavenly host praising God, and saying,

14Glory to God in the highest, and on earth peace, good will toward men.

Chapter Three

I t's not hard to live this new life I live now. I wake up and pull myself out of bed, perform a ritual of stretching exercises to loosen me up, either throw on a pair of sweat pants or Mother has bath ready for me to set myself into. Dad had just recently installed safety rails along side the tub I use. I'm learning to use them to get myself in and out from the tub as gracefully as I can. Lately I've discovered by sliding my left leg over the tub's edge first, then my right, it seems more natural.

If Mother's at work already, I make myself a light breakfast of cereal and toast, or I try my hand at actually cooking a real breakfast. I discovered though, that I need to constantly be cognizant of what I'm doing. The one time I cooked up some pancakes, I grabbed the handle, with my left hand, a little too close to the actual skillet itself and gave myself a nasty burn because my nerve endings aren't hyper sensitive anymore. I used to be able to react naturally to something like this. But now, my nerves don't respond to the same stimulus as before. I was watching my own hand begin to cook itself, and I wasn't able to remove my hand from the heat. I hurt like a son of a bitch, but I couldn't react like before. On her days off, she always cooks for us.

Some time during the day, during the week, the Home-Medics team arrives to do the physical and occupational therapy sessions that my insurance gladly pays 400 hours. At one point there were three women: one physical therapist to get me to walk, an occupational therapist to get my left hand and arm to start working and an older woman to give me baths. The bath lady decided after the first session she wasn't needed and resigned from my care. Now, Caroline, a vivacious thirty something blonde with a pretty smile handles all the leg exercises needed so I can retain balance, coordination and strength for standing and walking. Unfortunately, she's happily married. Lisa is an older woman in her late fifties, who works my hand to get it to respond to various stimuli, so if nothing else, can open and close my hand, so I can grasp stuff, then let go.

It's an effort because of the tone issues involved. When my hand and arm are totally relaxed, I can do pretty much anything I can set my mind to doing. But, the very moment the tone sets in, where all my muscles tighten or constrict, my hand and arm become a useless appendage. So, I try to do as little as possible with my left side and, in so doing, overcompensate by working my right side. I wear that stupid hand brace St Luke's gave me. I don't think it helps me any. Once I remove it, my hand automatically curls back. I can lay my hand flat on a counter or table top, stretching my hand muscles and tendons. That seems to help as well as wearing that brace.

Once a week, or every other week, I have appointments either with Dr. Stannic or Dr Morgan or someone else related to them in some fashion. They both have me on powerful drugs that puts me to sleep. They're muscle relaxants and anti-seizure medications. I can see using the one to keep my tone at bay, but as far as I know, I haven't had a seizure.

After the Home-Medics team leaves, I have the rest of the day for me. Most of me time is spent watching mindless TV while I stretch my arm on a rubber tubing, or going on my computer to read the latest news or go into my e-mails. Or I take walks around the house. Tyler and Cindy greet me as I walk slowly past their kennel. Cindy is a nine year old black Lab, and Tyler is a two year old long haired Dachshund. I'm usually greeted by two kittens that take great joy in playing around my feet as I attempt to maneuver around them. I don't know what it is, probably the quad cane I'm using, that they're so enthralled by.

Then Mother comes home from work around 4:30 and she prepares dinner for us. The rest of my night I stay in my room and watch TV until I have to get ready for bed.

It's not an overly exciting life by any stretch of the imagination. But, I have to say, it's a life none the less. Right now, I wouldn't trade it for anything. I'm thinking this in front of my computer as I prepare to scan over e-mails. Yes, this new life is boring. But, to me at least, it's more preferable than the alternative. I really don't know about life after death thing. I don't know if there really is a heaven or hell. All I really know for certain, when anybody dies, life ceases to exist. The physical body begins the natural cycle of decomposition, recycling itself to generate other life forms. Nature doesn't waste anything. I don't know about the spirit or the heavenly bodies. It makes for good reading in the Bible and other religious tomes. I don't know about God or Jesus, the prophets or the saints. I just know I'm not ready to find out right now. The way I see it, I have plenty of time to find out about these things, and garner the faith necessary to believe these things.

Do I really want to believe some of these things? Is the sixty four dollar question. I've been perfectly happy to criticize those that believe these things to the point of literal truth. I see many of these people as ignorant. They're version of what is truth is so beyond the pale as being beyond logic. Or, as Spock from Star Trek would say, illogical. I laugh at their belief system that criminalizes a woman's legal right to choose to terminate an unwanted pregnancy, or supports a State's right to kill a killer. What can I say? I'm probably their worse enemy. They more than likely see me as a traitor and a sinner. They most likely see the political party and philosophy I support as inherently evil. Do I dare tell my friends my true feelings or beliefs? How can I form such opinions around here? After all, as I mentioned earlier, this is God's Country. People of my like mind don't live on this side of the State.

I'm sitting in a bar in Pasco and someone comes up to me and asks to shoot a game of pool with him. While I shoot, he ask me what I think of Mexicans. I look at him. He's early to mid twenties, white with brown hair and reasonably straight nose. "I find them extremely friendly, hard working people who want very much to be respected in this country."

"Your one of those liberals, aren't you?"

"Yeah, but you asked me a question that required an honest and straight forward answer. And I gave it to you. Or did you want me to lie and tell you what you wanted to hear?"

He picks up his pool cue, puts it back in the cue rack and leaves.

There's also this other time, in West Richland, where I walk into a local bar and sit down for my customary after-work beer. A man, I never met is sitting down the bar from me and is apparently several beers ahead of me. He moves over next to me holding the local newspaper. "I want to show you something", "he sputters. It's a photo of two football players engaged in a tackle during a game. I try to read what the caption states, when he pulls it from my line-of-sight, and asks, "What do you see?"

"Well, from what little I could see, it was a picture of two football players one tackling another."

"Wrong! It's a picture of a white boy taking out a nigger."

"I don't appreciate that language around me. Why don't you go back over there and leave me alone."

"You some kind of nigger lover or something?"

"You don't even know me, and your talking shit to me. Maybe I am. I personally think it's none of your Goddamn business. So do us both a favor and leave me the fuck alone."

"Okay Joe," Jill cuts in. "Go over there and leave him alone. Your not in North Idaho and not everyone thinks like you here."

There were a lot more times, than I could think, where I held my tongue. The National Guard is the worse because I'm clearly in the minority here.

It's 1992 and we're heading up to Yakima Firing Center on a charter bus. I'll call him Corporal Rubenstein. He's getting liquored up for no apparent reason, other than he might be pissed off at something. "I think Bush needs to be reelected," he announces to everyone on the bus. "I'll kick whoever's ass if any of you vote for that fucker Clinton. He'll ruin this country so fast. He'll probably disband the military and legalize pot. The son of a bitch!" Rubenstein continues to rant about what an asshole Bill Clinton is and how great George H.W. Bush is. All the while I have to listen to this and keep my mouth shut because he's so drunk, anything I say to contradict him, would end up in a fight. I say to myself, 'look asshole, I'll vote for whomever I damn well please. Your drunken ass isn't going to intimidate me.'

Political and philosophical differences aside, I've enjoyed being in the National Guard. It's the one thing I know will have something for me when I reach retirement age. I can't honestly say that about my 401k plan, or Social Security, for that matter. Not when you have the present President Bush invading Social Security to pay for his tax cuts to the rich.

It's also a certainty I'll be back to work soon. I applied for Social Security disability the other day. The nice lady there asked me," Are you planning on returning to work full time?"

I think she expected me to respond "no." But instead, I said, "I very much want to go back to work. "I've heard from some of my friends, disability by itself doesn't pay very well."

"That's true. And with the present administration cutting benefits, it may not pay that well down the road either."

"Then, it's definitely no. I'm going to go back to work as soon as I'm physically able."

That's why I've always believed more in line to the Democrats than the Republicans. Democrats, when they cut certain programs, it's to cut out waste. Democrats raise taxes on the wealthy because they can afford to be taxed. Republicans cut into programs they philosophically don't agree with, like Medicare and Social Security. Then they cut taxes on the rich to feed their campaign war chests *come* election time. That's where I'm at now.

It's towards the end of January now. My progress is much more pronounced. Caroline and Lisa appear pleased that I'm slowly advancing toward a goal. Today, I'm going to inform them what the goal I set for myself. I don't see it as being out of reach. I see it as a milepost to past on the highway of life. All I'm doing is putting myself back on the road again. I have no intention of staying home indefinitely. I know some people may be that way, but not me. I want to go back to work as soon as I am able. As far as I'm concern I still have a job at the casino, under what capacity I don't know.

I feel my mind is slowly working its way back to some form of normalcy. On that point I continue to exercise my brain by writing and reading e-mails to my sisters and friends and keeping tabs to myself on where my crew is on this particular day because the nature of the rotating schedule at work. I read my Golf magazine trying to get pointers from the pros on optimizing my game.

I've increased my physical stamina and coordination, so I can walk to the end of Bluebird Way and back down to my driveway. I've even figured out a way to negotiate my way down to the three percent slope that leads down the driveway towards the garage. I'm able to open the trunk of my Intrepid and pull my wedges out to practice chipping and pitching. I wish I had made myself a putting green last year.

I also wish I didn't have to take these pills too. But, after forgetting to get them refilled the other day, causing my tone to dramatically increase, to the point where I could barely walk on my quad-cane and my left arm became totally useless because it had taken a position akin to a broken wing on a bird. Mother and I made sure to allow that to happen again. The part I hate about taking these meds, apart from the fact I can't touch alcohol anymore, is they make me so tired and listless. I feel I sleep a lot. And Dr. Stannic wants me to take them four times a day! That I feel is too much and informed her Medical Assistant that it was way too much and why. "You'll eventually get used to it Jack."

Well tell that to the family of the person I hit because I fell asleep at the wheel, I tell myself. I'm sure she'll most likely inform me I don't have a license to drive anyway, and therefore shouldn't even be driving. But, that's besides the point. But, realized it's not. That's my next goal, after getting back to work, to get my license back.

They arrive just as I'm finishing up making myself breakfast. They both smile at me as they enter the threshold. "Jack, how the heck are you today," Lisa asks with genuine enthusiasm in her voice.

"I'm doing great. I have made a decision."

"And what would that be?" Caroline asks suspiciously.

"It's not anything perverted," I try to assure her. "Though that has crossed my mind on occasion."

"Oh, whatever Jack. Tell us your earth shattering decision before we get started."

"I think I'm ready to go back to work in another month. It's something I've wanted to do since I left St Luke's."

I try to read something in their body language, but get nothing from them. "You realized we won't be able to provide therapy to you when that happens," Lisa informs me.

"I'll be heart broken, of course. But, this wasn't going to be forever anyway."

"We pretty much knew that," Caroline replied. "What are you going to do there? It's obvious you'll be limited, at least temporarily, on what tasks you can perform there."

"I'll find out. I know there's things I can do other than janitorial. I'll make some phone calls and find out."

It only takes one call, to my supervisor Roger, to receive the answer to her question. He's very pleasant and understanding to the question I pose to him. He responds quickly, "Jack, right now you could work at cleaning ash trays, like you did before. I'm certain you can handle that without too much difficulty."

"Alright Roger, thank you for your input. I'll pass this on to my case worker and physical therapist."

"Glad I could be of some help Jack. We'll be looking forward to seeing you back."

I can't help but grin as I hang up the cordless phone. "He said I could wash ash trays from a dish washer we have. It's really quite repetitious work, but easy to do."

"Jack, are you sure you want to do this? If you get fired you can't come back here to us again."

"I understand that. But, please understand yourself, I can't afford to give up. It's not in my makeup to give up. It's just not an option to me."

They both appear genuinely impressed with my response. "I guess then we need to set up some exercises for you so the concept will not be altogether foreign to you," Lisa states. "Now show me how you do this job."

"To start with there are two different kinds of ash trays that I need to wash every day. It basically is a two inch diameter ashtray and a four inch diameter size . . . The two inch type is about two inches high with the notches that hold the cigarette in set on that outer wall. The four inch ashtray is about half an inch in height, with an inner ring with four grooves that the cigarette can set in."

I watch for any glazing to occur, but to my surprise they appear interested in my lesson so far. So I continue, "The dish machine is pretty basic and has no complicated controls; raise the hood up, slide the full tray of dirty ashtrays into the machine, close the hood, and it starts automatically. After about two or three minutes the machine runs its cycle and stops. I pull up the hood, grab a dry towel and dry the ashtrays, stacking them in a cart for the next morning."

"It doesn't sound hard, like you said. So, show me how you would load them."

"I suppose, it would be like this. I would set about loading the dish rack with dirty ash trays, like this. I would need to load with my right hand to save on time."

"But Jack, doesn't that tend to defeat the purpose of your physical therapy? The goal is for you to regain use in your affected hand and arm.

Not to make your job more convenient by using your right hand and arm exclusively."

"I know that. But, I need to make money and be a productive member of my crew. To me it's not just about being able to use both hands and legs seamlessly, It's about being able to work effectively."

"That's not what we're about. Caroline is sounding more frustrated, and I make light of it and appear to give in.

"I'm just teasing with you two. Of course I'll be able to do the whole approach to work both my arms and legs, as much as I possibly can."

"That's better, Jack." With that she begins our therapy in earnest. It's tough to adjust the size and weight my dishes possess, in comparison to the ashtrays at work. "But Jack," Caroline persists, "wouldn't it be better to have heavier items here to work with? Then you won't be hampered with these smaller ashtrays."

I think about what she's saying, but it's not making sense to me; I keep my mouth shut, though. I already seem to be able to piss her off with little effort, so I better just be quiet about it. I'm thinking, though that I should be working with something closer to the real thing, than with something that is heavier or bigger than what I'm used to. As it is, I'm dropping saucers and bowls on the linoleum floor. Fortunately, none break, though it's possible they could have.

A few days later, I'm riding with Mother from the Moose Lodge. It's funny how I'm treated there, as opposed to other places, but that's for another time. As we round the curve, at the top of Big Sandy, I notice a sign at a vacant building that used to be a video rental stating a new physical therapy would be opening soon. I'm more than just a little interested in this, since most physical therapy businesses are in Spokane.

"Looks like someone is opening a clinic for physical therapy," I tell her as she drives past the sign.

"Are you going to do physical therapy there then?"

"I don't see why not. We can do it until the insurance tells us to stop."

"Do you want to stop by there tomorrow to check it out?"

"Yeah, let's do that."

Mother picks me up the next morning after she arrives from work. It's a mild February day and I get inside. The place is bare except for a desk, a couple of chairs, two padded tables one could lay on, and a few pieces of exercise equipment. A short, athletic oriental man greets me.

"Hey there, I'm Frank and this will eventually become Phase One physical therapy."

I'm Jack, and this my mother . . ."

You don't need to introduce Mary! We go way back when I was working at Shiners' Hospital."

They hug briefly. "So you're going to try and make a go of it then, "Mother asks.

"Yeah, I thought I need to try to make real money for a change. I see you're still working at Shiners' yourself. You must be getting ready to retire yourself then."

"Not just yet. My husband's retired and I need to work to keep him on some medical plan."

"I see. Okay, then what do I owe this privilege?"

"I suffered a stroke a couple months ago, and am in need of a physical therapist."

"Do you have home care?"

"Yeah, but they'll be done with me by the end of the month. I'm going back to work, and they can't give me home care once I return back to work."

"Lori will be happy to give you the necessary paperwork to fill out. Who's your insurer?"

"Premiera," I reply.

It's a few days later when I have this idea to take the bus to the casino. I'm thinking that I need some indication how long it actually takes to ride the transit. It's not the first time I've ridden a bus in this town, but it will be the first time I've taken the bus to the casino.

I talk with Mother about my idea. "It sounds good to me. Are you planning to buy yourself a bus pass too?" I tell her this on the way to town. It's El Nino sunny and warm for February. At least the weather is nice for doing this sort of thing.

"No, I wasn't planning to. I just want to get some kind of indication how long it takes to go from the stop up at this Circle K store up here, to the casino, and back." I mean, I have no idea what to expect here. For all I know I could take all day.

"So, you want me to drop you off up here at this store then?"

"Yeah, then I'll call you to pick me up some time this evening."

"Well, wouldn't it be better to drop you off at the main Plaza?

I planned to drive you home after I get off work anyway."

"I know, but it won't take that long from the plaza. I kind of want to get a time line set up, in case I should need to get hold of Dad to come and pick me up."

"Trust me, Jack. He won't pick you up. He'll tell you wait wherever for me to pick you up He's convinced this is a bad idea; you going back to work."

"I'm surprised. I would think, with his conservative nature he would be all for me getting back to the work force to avoid the stigma off being on public assistance."

"He supports that all right. He doesn't want you to be set up for failure. Or, worse in his mind, treated differently than anyone else because of your disability; giving your boss a reason to fire you because you can't pull your own weight."

"That won't happen because I won't let it happen. I plan to work just as hard, maybe harder than anyone else to prove I can pull my own weight."

We're at the convenience store, and Mother watches me get out of the Intrepid and close the door. I'm sure she's still watching me as I get onboard the bus colored in the official color scheme of Expo '74. They're not ugly colors; fairly normal, green to represent the trees and surrounding hills, blue to represent water, such as the many lakes and rivers in and around here, and white which I'm not certain what that color represent; perhaps purity. I slowly make my way to the bus using my quad cane, while the bus driver stands along side his bus smoking a cigarette. I try to make an attempt at levity. "Is this the express to Northern Quest Casino?"

But apparently, either he has the sense of humor of a toad, or he just wasn't in the mood."

"That's the 165 to Airway Heights. We don't got an express out there, just to Cheney and Liberty Lake." He's somewhere in his mid to late thirties has his long black hair pulled back in a ponytail. He wears a knock off pair of Ray-Bans, and he has his generic pack of cigarettes sitting inside the left breast pocket of his sky blue Spokane Transit Authority uniform shirt. I would think the company would supply the drivers with ties, but I think that's not part of the uniform here. Even though I think it would accent the uniform quite well. They would definitely look more professional. He also sports a handlebar mustache.

I sit in the seat reserved for old people and the handicapped. At this point I'm quite comfortable here. I watch him pull his body into the drivers' seat. He presses a button to start the diesel engine. He shifts the transmission lever to drive, presses another button that activates the left turn signal and we're off on my fun adventure to Northern Quest Casino.

I'm the only passenger for the better part of ten or eleven blocks before he picks up a couple teenage girls, most likely playing hooky. The bus moves through a quiet suburban neighborhood, seemingly upper middle class and very Republican. We then move onto the Nine Mile Road, hang a right and roll up to Driscoe, which is still a decent and quiet neighborhood. I don't how much Republican it is though. It's definitely not upper middle class, but, rather moderately middle class. It's where store managers and car salesmen live, as opposed to store owners or district sales managers where we just came from.

It's not long before we move into more working class neighborhoods where trades people, such as electricians and mechanics live. They're moderately successful, but like most neighborhoods, are most vulnerable to the whims of the local and national economy. We pick up a few more passengers along the way. Most seem to be young teenagers just getting off from school, some are retirees going to the market to pick up their weekly ration of groceries. And a very select few are working people heading to their jobs. After all, this is still the Western United States, where if you don't have a car, you're a failure.

So people that can barely afford to keep their family fed, have fifteen to twenty year old cars, that are untuned or ill-timed, spending their paychecks on keeping the car in gas so they can go to work and not feel like a failure. There are those people, who work and either can't have a car or couldn't have a car if they wanted to because they lost their driving privileges or because of mental or physical defect. These are the working poor who tend have the jobs no one else wants. They mostly live in either South-Central Neighborhood, also known as Felony Flats, or North-East Spokane, also know as Hillyard. This day though, this bus just skirts the outer boundary of Felony Flats, crossing across Northwest Boulevard to C.J. Minnoch Avenue, I can see the older Victorian bungalow style homes that inhabit this older neighborhood. The bus crosses the Spokane River and meanders up hill to Fort George Wright Boulevard. Spokane Falls Community College, which used to be an Army base until just after the First World War.

The community college shares many of the buildings, such as the barracks and the commandant's residence, of the former fort. Most of the campus though, is occupied by buildings built within the last fifty years. I've never been on the campus, but I'm sure it's like most small campuses, such as an administration building, a science building, English, or humanities building and some form of social sciences building. And I'm sure there's a gymnasium and auditorium too. We stop at the kiosk and pick up a group of students and move on to the residence that holds a large group of Japanese exchange students. They're mostly nineteen and twenty year old women who come here to become teachers.

Several years ago, there was the scandal involving two of the girls. They were waiting for the bus at the stop located on Fort George Wright Boulevard, when a young woman offered them a ride. The girls innocently accepted her offer. She then drove the girls to a house, where a group of men were apparently waiting for them. They all belonged to a Dominant & Submission cult. The girls were blind-folded and forced to drink some sort of intoxicant, where they were stripped of their clothes, made to perform a variety of sexually perverted acts, including bound and chained, oral sex on each other and the men, sodomy and rape. Thus the reason the bus now pulls up to the dormitory, where the oriental girls are picked up.

The bus then proceeds to Government Way, go pass a huge church, then by a pair of cemeteries where the graves are covered by shadows of tree branches from pine and spruce and Oak and Maple. The bus meanders on to Riverside. This street will runs us into the Peaceful Valley neighborhood then just outside Browne's Addition, and in the Downtown area, where high rise buildings and a myriad of businesses now occupy my vision. The bus pulls up to the Plaza, where all the other busses, sticking to a strict schedule, pull up to debus it's passengers. It's filled with any number of humanity. From those like myself, hobbling about to reach my next bus, to teenagers and transients needing a place to hang out, to business professionals taking advantage of the skywalk network, which this is a part, to security and police officers watching everyone in this post-9/11 atmosphere.

I go to an electronic message board that shows the arrivals and departures of all busses I count twenty or more routes that cover most of Greater Spokane. I finally locate my next bus, and it's leaving real soon. So I get motivated to hobble myself and my quad cane to the Sprague side of the plaza. Normally, it probably would have taken two minutes to walk the distance needed, but now I'm certain it takes at least twice that long. So, when I get to where that bus is, it's just leaving. Now I have to wait twenty five minutes for the next bus.

I walk back inside and sit at the nearest stool, which is a greenish marble colored thing. I sit next to a bum that asks if I have a cigarette.

"No, I quit two months ago." Or has it been three months? Time is flying by faster than I like.

"Why you walking with that cane for?" His accent is maybe mid western, I'm not sure. He sounds uneducated as much as anything; like he spent high school in the parking lot drinking beer or fortified wine.

"I had a stroke back in November."

"Oh, what the hell caused that?"

"Too much drinking."

Oh, bullshit. You don't get stroke from drinking." He looks defiantly at me. He acts like I just insulted his intelligence.

"I used to think that way too," I replied to him calmly. "I can't explain it any better to you. When I drank, it elevated my blood pressure, and when I had my stroke, I was drinking at the time. A blood vessel burst in my brain, called a hemorrhagic stroke."

"Oh, I didn't know that. Well, you appear to get along okay," his voice softens. "God bless you." He smiles briefly, exposing two top teeth and four bottom teeth, all yellow and decaying.

I sit alone now with everyone around me making conversation to each other or talking on their cell phones, or rushing to catch their bus.

I watch the reader board as arrivals and departures are posted and removed at the appropriate times. Finally my bus arrives and I make my way to the bus and board it. Many more people get on this bus. It's apparently a very popular route. I'm not sure why, though. It's not long before the bus is full and the driver pulls out, on schedule, along with the ten other busses that arrived to pick up passengers a couple minutes before.

To my surprise I here Joan call me from the seat behind me. "Jack, what are you doing?"

"Not much, Joan; I'm going to Airway Heights to get an idea how long it takes to get to work from Seven Mile."

"Are you going back to work then?"

"Yes, starting next Monday."

"You know I got the donations for you at work going?"

"Really? I wasn't aware," I reply honestly. She also works on my housekeeping crew. She appears nice and pleasant to be around. I'm still not sure I can trust her. She's short and petite, probably no more than 110 pounds soaking wet. She's strictly working class, with all the normal hang ups that working class types have, such as an inferiority complex and loathing towards authority figures and minorities. She's nice towards me, but I often wonder if there is some ulterior motive behind that. She never discuss her political views, but I think that is due to the fact that she knows her views, if known, would make her look ignorant. She's mid forties and somewhat pretty. She keeps herself clean, and I'm sure her house is clean too.

"Yes, I felt bad for you and realized no one else was doing anything for you, so I went and talked to that one lady who works upstairs."

"Yeah, she got hold of me, to get permission to do that."

"Cool. Well, you look great. This is my husband, Tom."

"Nice to meet you," I offer my right hand as I twist myself to reach around."

"Don't bother hurting yourself to be polite," Tom states gruffly. So I put my right arm down.

"What brought you here today?" I ask to be polite.

"He had an appointment to see Social Security," Joan replies. Tom remains quiet. I turn back around and watch the scenery go by at 60 miles per hour as the bus moves up Sunset Hill. Before too long the bus veers off I-90 and onto US-2 towards Airway Heights. The town is very much a Base town, since it's only a couple miles from Fairchild Air Force Base. There really isn't much else here. I think, if it wasn't for the base, and to some extent, the casino, this town would dry up and go away.

After a bit, we turn at Hayford Road. After a mile or so, we reach the casino. Rather than get out, I elect to stay on board. We're just going to the base and back here. Little did I know, the base isn't the only leg to this journey. The bus went to the base alright, but also, we went to Medical Lake. It's a backwater town that, if it wasn't for the base, and the State Mental Hospital, wouldn't exist. There isn't any other industry here. I guess there's farms around the town that I believe grow wheat, but not altogether certain. I'm taken on a grand tour of this town; the welcome sign show a population of 12,000. I don't know how accurate that is.

I do know the high school is right at the beginning of the town's business area, along with the football stadium and track. There's a grocery store across the street from the high school. We go down the main drag as far as a pizza parlor, then we turn off to a street, or road, if you will, that meanders to the main entrance of the state mental hospital, where we pick up three staff members. The building is definitely a pre-depression era design, perhaps early twenties. It has that neo-Gothic look that reminds me of a Frankensteinian movie set. There's a set of towers on either side of the facade, along with a granite slab with "Eastern Washington Hospital" sculptured out to advertise its purpose.

It's all red brick, in serious need of a good power wash to take away the blackened tint that has accumulated over these many years. There are windows, but I don't see any evidence that they open; more than likely it's that double or triple pane tempered glass that saves energy.

We then head back through Medical Lake, passing by the names sake water hole. The water is placid and the late afternoon sun reflects invitingly off the still water. If it wasn't for the time of year, this would be a nice place to fish. Two of the Medical Lake staff pull the cord and are let out just before we leave the city limits sign.

We stop at the Yokes Store in Airway Heights. The driver gets out and walks to the store. Where the hell is he going? Obviously, he's taking a break. But why now? I can't believe this. I try to call Mother to inform her of this latest twist to this road trip. But the phone won't unlock, and as is my luck, can't get hold of her. I feel like a hostage now. This wasn't part of the plan. I guess I should have stayed at the casino. I'd be well on my way back home now.

Apparently, the other passenger is used to this and has closed his eyes to take a nap. Twenty minutes go by before the driver slowly ambles his way back to the bus. While he was gone, two other passengers arrive and wait patiently for him to return. He goes into his driver seat and collects the fares from the new passengers. He pulls the bus out then head towards the casino. But rather than stop at the casino, we go right pass it. Now where is he taking us? We stop by the Airway Heights Prison that many people, including me, mistakenly believe is called Geiger. This is actually a medium security prison run by the State.

Geiger is a county jail that is located near the Airport. The driver moves the bus around a parking lot, then we move back to the casino.

The sun is sinking fast. I check the time and it's quarter past four. It will be dark soon, and I'm no closer to home than I was an hour ago. I can't believe I could be so wrong about this. I'm totally seething now. The idea I could do this whole adventure in a couple hours is a joke. I can only imagine what Mom and Dad are thinking now.

Fortunately, there are no more stops and the bus moves down Highway 2 and onto the Interstate, exits at Lincoln street and we finally arrive at the Plaza. I get out and head inside to see that I've just missed the number 20 going to Seven Mile. So I have to wait again for my connecting route. The cell phone rings. I hit the green button, and to my surprise it connects. It's Dad.

"Where are you?"

"I just now made it to the plaza." I want to explain to him about this trek I put myself through, but by the tone in his voice, I know better.

"When are you planning on getting home? I have a Goddamn meeting to get to and your mother isn't home yet!"

Then cook your own fucking meal. "I'm waiting on my connecting bus. It will be here in a couple minutes time." You asshole! He hangs up abruptly. I can't believe him. He treats Mom like his indentured servant, rather than his wife. He can't even cook his own meal for Christ sake. I sit on the bench fuming at myself and my father and that bus driver and this stupid schedule.

Ten minutes later, my bus arrives. I get on the Sprague Street side. We move out and the bus is packed full of commuters. The anti-transit people should come here now to gauge whether this place needs a bus system. Of course, they would come up with a different argument. I just have to laugh at these people because what it really boils down to is they hate paying taxes. They're so conservative, that they're actually anarchists who would be happiest with no government at all. Slowly the number of commuters whittles down to about three or four by the time I get to my stop. I assume that he's going to stop here for his coffee or cigarette break; he doesn't. We drive pass, and I have to pull the cord. The bus stops at the next stop, that's about two hundred yards down the street from the convenience store.

The cell phone rings and I answer it. It's Mother.

"Where are you?"

"I'm just down the street, I'll be up here real soon."

"Where down the street?"

I can see her in the phone kiosk. All she has to do is turn around and she can see me. "I'm right here Mom."

"Where?"

"Here, down the street from the store."

"Where?"

"Here! Turn around and look down the street."

She does. "What the hell are you doing down there?" She hangs up before I can respond.

"I tried calling earlier when I realized I'd be held up longer than anticipated, but I couldn't figure out the stupid lock on the phone."

"Well your father is probably pissed because he has a meeting to attend with the fire department tonight."

"I know, he called me."

We get into her Jeep Cherokee, although I still struggle a bit getting inside. Soon we're on the highway heading home. "Anyway, I got the gist of getting there and back, side trips notwithstanding. It takes about twenty minutes to get there and about the same amount coming back. It just depends on the number of stops that has to be made along the way. The earliest I can leave, according to the bus schedule, is 6:05, and that will get me there around six fifty."

"So, in other words, I'll have to drop you off at the bus stop in town on my way to work, so you can get your butt to work on time."

She makes it sound like such an inconvenience. "It's on your way to work Mom. It's not like I'm making you go out to the Valley or something."

"It doesn't matter to me. How are you going to get home?"

"Well, obviously, I'll have to wait for you to get off work. The bus will drop me off at the plaza, then I'll just wait for you to get off."

We're quiet the rest of the way home. I don't notice the route anymore; I always take it and don't pay attention to its many nuances. How it meanders or how narrow it becomes. The highway that we take everyday and its many hidden dangers that I won't become aware of for many years to come.

Of course Dad is pissed off when we show up. "I've been waiting for my dinner for over an hour." I ignore him and go to my room to read a Golf magazine. But, I hear him bitching at Mother, "I don't understand what all this was about anyway. Going on a bus, why? He never tells me anything."

"He wanted to see how long it would take for him to get to work."

"They're not doing anything more than giving him lip service. What the hell can he do? He's fucking disabled."

"Warren, I've seen first hand that physical therapy and exercise does wonders to people like Jack. Within a year, you won't recognize him. What do you want for dinner?"

"I want a pan fried steak and baked potato."

"Any vegetables?"

"Have any carrots?"

"I'll have to look." I hear her rummaging in the pantry cupboard. "How about Peas and carrots?"

"That's fine." While the potato is in the microwave, she open a can of peas and carrots, throws them in a sauce pan and boils them. Then, because Dad likes his steak pink, she heats up the frying skillet, places the burner on high, and waits for the potato to finish baking before throwing the streak on the skillet. I can hear the meat sizzling in the cooking oil. It's a hot, violent sound. I can imagine the meat is turning brown to black just from the sound of the sizzling meat. Then silence, as she pulls the steak off the skillet and onto Dad's plate. All done in less than ten minutes, and he still makes it to the meeting on time.

Mother then cooks up a couple of hot dogs and chili for us after Dad has left. I just wonder how that man can sleep at night by the way he treats her. I guess Mother did raise me right after all.

Chapter Four

I t all seems like a dream to me; a weird, surrealistic dream in which I'm thrown under the bus and my whole world is thrown up-side-down. But, it's okay because my life prior to November 21, 2002 was seemingly meaningless. Sure I had accomplished a lot, such as earning my Eagle Scout award, graduating from high school and then college, and spending twenty plus years in the national guard, but this life was incomplete and wasted due to my bad choices in life:

"Jack, you wanna try this cigarette?"
"Sure, why not."
"Jack, you wanna beer?"
"Okay."
"Jack, you wanna hit from this joint?"
"Yeah."

Not once did I make a conscience choice to not do those things. I was a willing participant. I'm certain my life would have been drastically different had I said no to any, if not all, those offers in my life. But, then there is the other matter I have to contend with. I know in my heart and in my mind, I am very much capable being a leader of men. Yet, outside of Boy Scouts and two years in National Guard where I was a squad leader, I've been denied this opportunity. In the case of the National Guard, I was informed I wasn't assertive enough. I don't know if that's true, or an excuse because of my harelip and speech impediment. Or maybe they're just blowing smoke up my ass; that it's about brown nosing those people that actually make the final decision on whom they want in charge. It's apparent, at least in the National Guard, to be a good leader is to be outspoken, to a point and arrogant. They want you to tell it like it is to those beneath you, but don't do that to your superiors or you would be considered insubordinate. My approach was always treat everyone equally and fairly, no matter their rank or pedigree. But apparently, that's not the National Guards' idea of an ideal leader.

My mind is thinking this, a week before I'm to go to Gig Harbor to see my guard unit one last time. It's to be a very busy week for me because I'm also going to be going to work. We are going to Iraq starting next September. I won't of course. No one knows what our job will be there. The big fighting will most likely be done with by then. The actual invasion is set for March 17. We all know this; even Saddam. So why are we going? It's supposedly a two year commitment; one year training and one year in country. So, I'm thinking we are going there for the long haul; like Germany and South Korea. We have just committed ourselves to permanently being in that region for ever. So, in my mind, this foray of George Bush has nothing to do with fighting terrorism, and everything to do with spheres of influence. The real war on terrorism should be fought in Afghanistan. There are no terrorists in Iraq. That would be a real threat to Saddam's power. So all of this talk about Saddam and Iraq and the "axis of evil," is just talk; propaganda to get the U.N. behind us while we prepare for war and occupation.

Mother drops me off for work. It's 6:25 in the morning and I have to wait for the bus to take me to work. I wait a half hour when the I'm to ride arrives and I board. The driver is a young thirty something man with short brown hair and sunglasses. I place a dollar bill in the bill slot and sit down behind the driver. By 7:30 the bus drops me off at the north entrance. I then walk, with my quad cane around to the side entrance where employees have to go. It takes me about ten minutes to get there. I show the security officer my badge and I head to where our supply room is, but the place is empty. Where is everyone? The supervisor's desk is no longer there. Instead, a cabinet filled with cleaning chemicals occupy that space. The dish washer we use fore ashtrays is there. I could conceivably begin cleaning ashtrays, except I haven't signed in yet. The fact that I only work a certain number of hours makes it imperative that I sign in first. Then someone from B team shows up with a cart filled with dirty ashtrays. I see from his name on his badge he is Doug. The picture shows a full beard and curly brown hair. The photo had to been taken the day he was hired. This morning the beard is shaven and the curls are gone. "Can I help you?"

"Where's the supervisor?"

"He's in his office. Who are you?"

"I'm Jack. I'm here to do ashtrays for you guys."

Doug appears dubious. "I see. I don't know anything about that."

Apparently Roger and I are the only ones that do know. "So where do I need to go?"

"Four to Two Greg." Doug calls on the portable two way radio.

"Go ahead." Greg responds.

"Some guy is here looking for you."

"Who?"

"He says he's here to clean ashtrays."

"I don't know anything about it. Bring him to the supervisor's office."

"Come with me." He places the radio on his belt, and I follow him to the new south expansion area. "Are you a new hire?"

"No, I worked here before for the past two years. I was gone these past four months because I suffered a stroke."

"Sorry to here that." We walk pass employees' restrooms by a office, then the maintenance room, and beside that, housekeeping office. Greg is sitting behind his desk. "Doug, why didn't you tell me it was Jack?"

"I don't know," he replies, then leaves.

"That guy is a real idiot. I don't see him lasting very long around here," Greg says more to himself than to me. "How the Hell are you?" He grabs my right hand and gives it a firm hard shake.

"I'm doing good," I reply. Greg is somewhere in his fifties and got hired last year. He has experience from Kaiser, like Roger. He has a full head of salt and pepper hair, and the lines on his hair are very clear and deep. He's a couple inches taller than me, but stockier with a solid beer gut. I'm sure he was quite the lady's man in his day. "I guess I just missed seeing Roger so he could explain what was going on."

"No, he told us what you two had concocted." He eyes me for a moment. "You know you don't have to do anything. I have Christy here who washes ashtrays. If you want to just stand around and watch her, you'd still get paid for your time here."

Are you serious? "No, I need to know I can do this."

"Okay, then. Come with me and I'll get you started."

"I follow him back to the supply room where I proceed to get started washing ashtrays. As I described to Lisa and

Caroline, the work is not hard. It's repetitive and boring. I tend to play songs in my mind to at least occupy my brain with something other than watching left hand hold the ashtray while my right hand wiped the blackened tar off its surface. There's a new wrinkle to the equation too, besides the fact that there's a whole new area that we have to work, we're responsible for cup holders too. These are clear plastic with an extended bottom to wedge the holder into the black imitation leather cushion the customers lean against.

I don't know if these things actually get so dirty that we have to pull them every 24 hours, but I don't know what customers actually use these things for other than holding paper cups. The whole ashtray cleaning process takes me approximately three hours to complete. I'm supposed to be here for four, so I have to start finding other things to do. So I try and wash out the large 60 gallon trash cans that are connected to a set of four castors. They're quite deep and I struggle to clean the very bottom of the can. There are brushes that I use, that seem to help, but then I still need something that I can easily dry it clean. I finally come up with a mop handle and wrap the absorbent cloth towel to capture the excess water.

I'm done at around noon and I grab a quick bite before heading to the bus stop. I feel I put in a full days work, though it was only four hours. I find a place in the employee dining room, or EDR, that is close to where I can get food and be out of every ones' way. I get in line with my quad cane in one hand and realize, that this is going to be an effort. One of my coworkers seems to recognize my plight and others to get my food for me. "Sure, thanks," I reply to his offer for help.

"Ok then, you want salad?"

"Yeah, about that much lettuce, some broccoli, carrots, and tomatoes; that's good."

"Soup?"

"No, not today. Let's move to the main course. I'll have the chicken, the rice, and I guess that will do for now. Thanks for your help."

"No problem, I'm glad that you're here to get me to help you."

"Okay, I'm not sure I quite understand what you just said, but thanks for the compliment." He's dark hair and brown eyes and mildly brown skin. He has fairly large, big bone features that define his body, including a gut that makes it appear he's eight months pregnant. He's maybe a couple of inches taller than me. His uniform tells me he's in slots. He smiles broadly at me showing uneven teeth that needs serious cleaning.

"That didn't come out right. I know. Let me try again. I saw your picture a couple months ago wanting donations to help pay expenses. I think you making the effort to come back to work is quite remarkable."

"Well thank you for the vote of confidence. I feel I need to come back just to show I not broke down."

Just as I'm getting over to where I'm going to sit though, another group of people come in and take over my spot.

"Excuse me, but I'm sitting here."

"Well, we always sit here. You will have to find yourself another place to sit." This guy seems a bit effeminate, with all characteristics that define a native, including his arrogance. He's from the Camas Institute, an organization that the tribe set up to teach natives to read and write. They also provide drug and alcohol counseling. I take an instant dislike to this guy. Then he sees I'm disabled and grabs my stuff and food for me and puts me somewhere else. I want very much to cause a scene here and embarrass the hell out of this bastard, but hold my tongue and sit where he put me.

I go home with that last scene being played out in my head. I know he can't help himself, like Republicans can't help their ignorant selves. He's so full of himself, he can't see what his problem is. And of course, everyone else around him just ignore his stupidity and pretend nothing really happened. I just know the bastard embarrassed me and made me feel like his fucking lap dog. "No, you can't sit there!" I want to slap his arrogant face in front of everyone there. But I would have been fired. But, damn, it would have felt good doing it. I just have no use for arrogant people who feel all so superior, when in reality, they still have to drop their pants and sit on the toilet to take a crap like everyone else.

I sleep well on the bus and at the Plaza. Mother is there at around four, though she claims she clocks out at 3:30. We talk of our day at work. She also has issues with coworkers who have it in their minds how ultimately superior they are to her because she is just another housekeeper. "It must be our station in life Mom."

"I'm afraid it is. We just have to remember, that we all are the same under the eyes of God."

I mull on that a bit. But what if God is like us? Wouldn't He feel superior too to certain people? Then that would mean He is no better than the rest of us. I fall asleep while on the road to home and don't wake up until we get to the turnoff where the highway's pavement becomes Whitmore Road's gravel and washboard surface. Dad is in his recliner watching the TV; some NRA show on the Outdoor Channel. At least the host is talking about the evils of gun regulation and how the Democratic Party is bent on the path of outlawing guns.

I know this is another lie from Republicans but I keep this to myself since Dad is an orthodox Conservative Republican. Yet, I noticed lately, now that G.W. is talking about preemptive warfare against Iraq, he's been unusually quiet about it. I don't think he is really all that favorable about the course this country is going either. I don't think he likes Rumsfeld or Cheney either. They don't appear to embrace the Reagan Doctrine of less intrusive government. Since 9/11, the focus appears to be more on making our government being bigger and more intrusive.

The month seemingly goes by without a hitch. I arrive at work around eight each morning because I can't seem to make it any earlier. I hate being treated differently than anyone else. Yet, it appears everyone wants to help me do something, though most of the time they haven't a clue what it is they need to do. I patiently tell them that everything is fine. I know my limitations, but many of these people don't appear to believe I can do anything. It's almost like they really don't want me here at all, but are too politically correct to tell me that to my face. Instead they act nice to me and offer to help me.

March is gone and April is here. Life, for some reason continues its merry course toward an unknown future. I increased my time at work from four hours per day to six. I increase my workload there from strictly washing ashtrays to washing ashtrays and cleaning trash cans.

In other areas, I'm slowly paying off the hospital bills. It appears everything is in apple pie order, except for this one nagging issue with a certain anesthesiologist that keeps nagging me about the hernia surgery I had done June of the previous year. I try calling these people up to find out what this bill is about since as far as I'm concerned the National Guard should be picking up the tab.

Finally, I get a bill stating I must pay this or it would go to collections. Once again I attempt to contact them over the phone and only get voice mail. Once I hear the metallic beep after the perfunctory instructions to leave a message, I let loose. "Yes this is Jack and I don't know what's going on. I've been trying to get hold of you to find out. I don't know what the hell's going on. Just cease and desist calling me again unless your willing to be standing by the phone to get information."

I hang up, not knowing for certain where this outburst will lead. But I'm certain nothing good will come out of this. I feel much better though. I should have done this months ago, but didn't. Well actually I did. The incident that aggravated my hernia happened while on duty on drill weekend.

We are on our tank, M1A1, suddenly broke down. We hook up to a M-88(Mike-88) Recovery vehicle. We load up inside the recovery vehicle and settle down in back. We're soon asleep from the vibrating rumblings from the tracks crunching the gravel road. Something very strange is happening; suddenly brakes are applied. I feel the tracks are leaving the road and we feel ourselves losing our equilibrium. I instinctively move my left foot to balance myself.

We're stopped now. The tank commander opens the side hatch and we exit. It's all adrenaline now. We see the damage and the potential of what could have happened. The Mike 88 driver apparently loses control when the momentum from the heavier tank pushes the recovery vehicle down the road at a dangerous speed. He pulls the vehicle off the road to avoid going completely out of control and causing more damage or injury. Just 50 feet further is a 100 foot drop off. The recovery vehicle's tow hook is broke. The only reason the tank didn't continue down the drop off, is both vehicles jack knifed and ended catching in an embankment.

We walk up to the road and I'm sent down to direct traffic while we wait for emergency crews to arrive. As it so happened, because the recovery vehicle towed us, we had to be last in the column. So we sent out the distress call and waited for Our commander and Platoon leader to turn around and come back. Within twenty minutes they return at break neck speed, concern, and then relief when they see no one is seriously hurt.

I didn't notice I hurt myself until the swelling started on the right groin area the next day. Then I could see the swelling increase and the throbbing pain when I attempted to lift anything heavy or cumbersome.

I reported my injury to Mike and he sent me to a doctor at Fairchild Air Force Base. She saw the injury and referred me to a civilian surgeon in Spokane. He saw me, and got me on the operating table within a month.

The problem it seems is the people at Holy Family Hospital didn't know the circumstances related to my injury and sent the paperwork to my primary insurance carrier where I normally work. Whereas, it should have gone to my National Guard provider. Once I told them it wasn't Premier-Blue Cross, but Tri-Care instead, everything was back to being okay, except the anesthesiologist never received his money.

All this time, I pretty much assume anesthesiologists worked for the hospital, like radiologists. It never occurred to me they would have their own practice at some other place; that they worked independent of hospitals. So now I'm looking forward to getting sued for this guy who wants his money.

March drill will most likely be my last drill mostly because there isn't much left for me to do here. I can't physically climb aboard a tank, at least not safely. I don't see any possible job or role I could pursue that would satisfy my commitment here. I'm not even certain as to why exactly they want me here for this drill, except maybe to wish me happy trails.

All that I know for certain is that Mike called me the Monday before drill weekend to inform me my presence there was requested and required as per the First Sergeant. "Also, you're to bring all your doctors' reports and hospital records that pertain to this incident," he directs me in such a way that to not do so would be tantamount to treason, or insubordination.

I pack my stuff, with the expectation I would have to turn my gear and uniforms in; at least that's Mother's hope. Friday I have my two duffle bags and Alice pack and CVC bag with helmet full of uniforms and gear that Uncle Sam has issued me these pass twenty two years. Most of it has been replaced several times since a lot of the times I transfer units and am issued new equipment. Plus, I've had stuff stolen and I also have lost items too. I struggle to stuff everything into the Intrepid, using my one arm and right leg to try and haul this stuff from a camp trailer that sits in the back yard, to the driveway area some thirty yards away.

After work I meet Mother at the bus plaza, where she picks me up. "I need to pick up my records for the drill," I tell her. So she takes off, where I have no idea. She's heading north up Ruby before finally ask her where she's going. "To the hospital."

"No, Mother to Dr. Morgan's at the St. Luke's Rehab."

So she turns around and being it's Friday at 4pm, traffic is getting extremely heavy. Luckily I don't have to change into my uniform. But, I'm feeling like my stress level is getting to a all time high. We arrive by 4:30 and I make my way inside. Once I'm in her clinic, I go directly to the receptionist and ask for the records and the latest doctor's report related to my stroke.

"Did you call for them already?"

"No, I didn't realize I needed to."

"Yes, and the doctor won't release her reports without written authorization."

"But, they're my records, why can't I have copies?"

"It's not that easy. We need written authorization before we can release them. And, we require at lease four hours notice so we can gather them. Who are these for?"

"My national guard unit in Gig Harbor."

"Well, what we can do is give us the address and we'll mail them to your unit, once we receive authorization."

"Can I get that in writing?"

"Of course." She proceeds to write down what she had told me. The part about getting prior notice is definitely my fault. I should have contacted her Tuesday so I would have this ready for tonight. She hands me the information and I head towards the car.

Once I get inside, Mother asks, "Where the records that you so desperately needed?"

"I don't know. They say I need authorization or something. They're my records. I shouldn't need to have authorization."

"Well, where to now?"

"To the armory I guess."

"I've never been there. Where's it at?"

"It's on Geiger Road across from the airport."

It's almost 5pm now and traffic going up Sunset Hill is nearly at a standstill. We get to the Geiger exit and head up Geiger Road until we reach Electric Road and veer right. A guard is stationed at the gate and I show him my military ID. He allows us entry and the gate opens from left to right, it's chain driven motor humming along as the chains slap against the steel bars.

Once we're in front of our administration building I pull myself out of my car. Mother helps me unload the car. "Okay, Mother thanks and I'll see you some time Sunday, I think."

She leaves and I go up the flight of stairs that go up the outside building. Once I get up I go through a doorway and walk twelve feet down a hall to an office on the right where Mike is sitting behind a desk.

"Well, I have some good news and bad news, Sergeant Hunt."

"What's the good news?"

"Well, I'm here. Here's the bad news," I say as I hand him the sheet of paper the receptionist handed me.

He briefly reads over it then proceeds to open a memo window and up pops a template that authorizes them to gather records and reports on soldiers. He types out the necessary information and prints it out. Once it's printed, he hands it to me. "This should do it. If they have any questions, tell them to call me."

"I guess they want to mail that to you or whomever."

"Bring me back the authorization request."

I hand it back to him and he quickly writes down the address to the armory in Gig Harbor. He hands the authorization back to me and I place it in my jacket pocket. Sergeant Schmidt walks into Mike's office and greets me with a handshake and a smile. "It's good to see you back Jack."

"It's good to be back. Congratulations on your promotion."

"Well thanks Jack." He recently became a platoon Sergeant that included an additional rocker to his three chevrons. He looks tired. He teaches at an alternative high school in Coere d'Alene I can't recall what he teaches there; whether it's English lit or something else. He suddenly gets busy with the business of being a platoon sergeant in the National Guard.

I make my way further down the hallway towards where the lockers are and where some of my brothers in arms are getting ready. They greet me with a combination of curiosity and seeming indifference. Only about two or three are actual friends of mine. The rest are mere acquaintances who tend not to socialize outside drill weekends. They all wear their uniforms with their light blue berets to standard. Most are wearing light camouflage jackets with liner. They're clean shaven and have their hair cut well above the ears; some are practically bald with mere stubble on their heads. I tend to avoid falling into that trap of trying to out "GI" the other by cutting hair to stubble and the like. After all one still has to go back to work Monday with that haircut.

I walk back outside and attempt to climb my way down the stairway when one of my buddies asks if I need help getting down stairs.

"There's not much that you can do Specialist. Unless you want to build me an elevator."

He didn't quite know what to make of that comment. He couldn't see my facial expression to know whether I'm serious or kidding him. It appears he started to say something, but thought better of it and kept it to himself.

I move slowly, one step at a time. Until I make it to the landing where I move over to the road where we have our formations. I tend to stand in one spot and wait for the charter bus to arrive, allowing other people to congregate around me and pick up the conversations they may bring up. Talk anymore tends to center around what is about to happen and how we'll be deployed and when.

"I can't believe we aren't getting deployed now." Sergeant Rogers states to another sergeant and group of specialists.

"Hell, I hear the Texas Guard got deployed," Specialist Kennedy interjects between bites of a sandwich his wife made up for him before he kissed her goodbye.

"I think that has more to do with Bush and Cheney than with anything else," I reply.

"Oh you mean because they're from Texas," Sergeant Schmidt concludes. "That makes sense. How did you get that anyway Jack?"

"I'm not sure. What do you mean that?"

"Well, I heard you couldn't make it to drill. I just assume you caught flu bug or something. Now, I see you hobbling about and such like you were involved in an accident. What the hell happened?"

"I had a stroke." I figure that should explain everything, but it doesn't.

"Old people get strokes. You're not old."

"Obviously not, "I reply neutrally. "Anyone can get a stroke. I got mine because I drank too much. It affected my right brain, so now I'm half paralyzed on my left side."

"Well, it's cool your up and about. So you going to collect disability then?"

"Not only no, but Hell no. It don't pay but $800 a month. I can't live on that and expect to pay off my medical bills."

"Your back to work?"

"I'm slowly working my way back to full time status," I reply proudly.

"Well it's good to know you don't believe in government handouts. Not like these others on welfare who think the government owes them something when they haven't worked a day in their lives."

"These others you're referring to, who are they?"

"Damn crack whores, who give birth to crack babies. It's all Clinton's fault too. He's the one that started all this crap."

"Sergeant Schmidt, Clinton's no longer in office."

"And it's a good thing too. All he ever did was have sex in the oval office with that Lewpinski girl and smoke pot."

"I certainly wouldn't want him as our president now. He might use nukes and start a world war with China and Russia," Specialist Randall states in all seriousness.

They're all serious. They proudly express their conservative views on everyone here because it's assumed everybody in the National Guard, or part of the military establishment, are of like opinion. I'm not, and that's why I tend to keep my opinions to myself and not express what I feel or think.

"Hell, Clinton would have tried to find an excuse not to go to war. The Goddamn draft dodging, pot smoking adulterer anyway. Bush at least sees the logic of going to war against them sand niggers. They're ignorant for one, thinking we wouldn't go after them. For another, we're most important country in the world, and the greatest. How dare them assholes declare their Islamic jihad on us. And lastly, we just need a good war to rid this country of all the crack babies the crack whores brought into this world. Like Patton said, 'Americans love a good war.'"

Thankfully the charter bus arrives just in time, I feel, so I wouldn't have to listen to anymore from Sergeant Schmidt We're ordered to formation in front of the bus. We automatically assume the position of attention upon getting in line and dress-right-dress. Then we are ordered at ease by Sergeant Schmidt.

"Good evening gentlemen. Here's what the skinny is so far. We're heading to Gig Harbor in approximately ten minutes. We'll spend the night in the armory. Tomorrow morning we'll proceed to Fort Lewis and do our tank gunnery skills assessment tests. We are going to eat in the field then head towards Gig Harbor and sleep the night. Welcome back Sergeant Armstrong. If you don't already know, he suffered stroke last November. It looks like he's coming right along though.

"Platoon! Attention! Sir, do you have anything to add?"

Lieutenant George marches purposefully to the front of the formation where Sergeant Schmidt stands. A whispered cursory is exchanged before they salute each other and the platoon leader commands him "Post." Sergeant Schmidt right face goes to the back of the formation. Lieutenant George commands, "Platoon!"

Tank Commanders command in unison to their troops, "Squad!"

"Stand at . . ." from the Platoon Leader.

"Stand at . . ." rejoin the tank commanders.

"Ease." The platoon leader concludes. We proceed to go from standing at attention to moving our right leg thirty inches away from the left leg, and folding our arms behind our backs.

He's in his second year as platoon leader. He's intelligent looking and is attending law school at Gonzaga University. He has a myriad of conflicting opinions that I find refreshing. Such as he opposes capital punishment because it's generally considered not judicial justice, but, rather, vindication on the victims' families. "Men, as you most likely have heard, we're going to war against Iraq. I don't much care what your opinions are here because, let's face it, everybody has an opinion on this. When that day arrives that we'll be deployed, opinions will not deter us from performing our mission. We may not be deployed this go around, but when we do, I know we'll do our best, just as we always have.

"Sergeant, front and center." Sergeant Schmidt walks smartly to the front of the formation stands in front of Lieutenant George who commands him to proceed with loading the troops to the bus. They salute, the lieutenant right faces and moves ten paces away and to the back of the formation, while Sergeant Schmidt about faces. "Tank commanders, take charge of your troops and load them on the bus."

We load the bus. I'm pretty much helped on by two of my fellow soldiers and the bus driver, who sets an extra step in front of the bus to get in the entry. It's a clean bus with that familiar clean bus smell that includes a air freshener that comes standard on all buses. I sit in the seat behind the bus driver so I can be the first on to debus after the Platoon Sergeant and Platoon Leader who are always in the first seat on the right. The other soldiers file in behind with their CVC bags and other bags they bring along for this road trip.

It's a fairly straightforward trip from Spokane to Gig Harbor. We travel I-90 west to State Route 17 to Auburn. From there we go until reach the I-5 to Tacoma. Then we cross the Narrows Bridge and take State Route 120 north to Gig Harbor. There's a couple of streets through town we have to take, along with a round-about, where we make a right turn towards the Sound. The armory that is shared by a Navel Reserve unit sits on the right.

The Armory, such as it is, is a fairly old building built in the sixties. It was a elementary school that converted itself to an armory in the eighties. Two of the former classrooms became weapons' vaults. Naturally reinforcement had to be added to each classroom to make it secure, such lead lining, steel door with combination lock and high tech security system that has never been breached—mostly because no one has attempted such a daring stunt here. There's a gym with basketball hoops on either end, that in it's day also served as a auditorium because there is a stage that sits at the west end. No formations are conducted during our drills.

The cafeteria is still used for preparing and serving our chow. The majority of former classrooms are still used for that purpose, except two that has been turned into locker rooms for the soldiers' gear. The teachers' lounge is the First Sergeant's office. The Principal's office belongs to the Company Commander. The Executive Officers and Platoon Leaders share an office, while the Platoon Sergeants share another. Tank Commanders don't get offices.

The bus arrives here right on time, around one in the morning, which means those people that can't sleep on moving vehicles, will be dragging ass all day tomorrow. There's usually one or two individuals like that, and it always seems that take great pains to sit together and make just enough noise of conversation to keep most everyone else up.

We unload our gear and set up cots, for those that planned to sleep on cots; the rest of us roll out our sleeping bags on the hardwood floor on the stage. There is no talking now. All I hear before sleep finally overtakes me is the steady breathing or snoring of fellow soldiers.

Someone's alarm awakens us at 5:30. It's probably Sergeant Smith's. I struggle to pull myself up. I didn't undress before going to sleep. Sergeant Smith wanted me to sleep where I would be more comfortable. But no such place is available. "That's okay," I state. "I'll be fine on the floor."

Now I wish I could take back those words. I'm finally able to place myself into a push-up position and hoist myself up that way. I notice right away my folly though. As soon as I pat myself on this mini-victory, I look down at the sleeping bag I slept on earlier. "Shit."

"What's wrong?"

"I forgot to roll up my sleeping bag before I got myself up from the floor," I reply disgusted with myself.

"I got it," The soldier volunteers. He doesn't sound highly appreciative of his charity, and I don't blame him. "That's okay, I'll do it myself. I start to get back down on the floor to begin rolling my bag, when Sergeant Smith stops me.

"Let the PFC do it Sergeant Armstrong. That's his job, to help NCOs. Besides, the First Sergeant wants to see you."

"That doesn't sound encouraging."

"When is talking to the old man ever encouraging?"

"True." I gather the rest of my clothes and shoes and trudge over to the nearest chair. I put my brace and shoes on, followed by the sweatshirt I wore yesterday, and the light jacket. I get up and move over to the First Sergeant's office. He's sitting behind a desk, a very Spartan looking desk with inbox and computer monitor with keyboard. He looks like an old man with thinning gray hair and weathered face.

"How's it going Sergeant Armstrong?"

I always consider him a pretty up front man, but just by the way he greets me on this particular morning sends sirens blaring in my head. He greets me like I'm retarded; 'you're such a special person,' way that set me on edge. I can't trust him.

"I slept well First Sergeant," I reply looking at his rank on his lapels with a steady gaze.

"Did you bring that paperwork I requested?"

So that's what this as all about. "No, an authorization must first be sent from you to the doctor before any records are released. I too am puzzled by this, but I suppose they want to protect my privacy."

"Very well," he starts to write something on his notepad he has sitting in front of him.

"First Sergeant, Sergeant Hunt has already got the ball rolling on that."

"Very well then. I guess that's all I need you for then." I leave his office. An hour later, I'm heading back to Spokane with Sergeant Hunt, fuming at the First Sergeant. For a Christian man, he definitely knows how to cuss.

"That ignorant, self important son-of-a-bitch! He didn't believe you had a stroke, so he wanted you to travel three hundred miles to prove you aren't fit for duty. I told him, and the fuckin' Sergeant Major January told him, and Sergeant Smith told him. No, he insisted on dragging your ass down here. He's the worst fuckin' first sergeant I've ever had the displeasure of meeting or being around. God damn he fuckin' pissed me off!"

I just sat in the seat behind him as he drove the van at breakneck speed to get me back home. Eventually, he's finish ranting and venting. He starts quoting scripture about how Christ healed the sick and said how he placed that power in the hands of true believers. "I feel I can do that for you too Jack, if you'd let me."

I really don't care. It's all a bunch of hocus-pocus anyway. So he thinks he has the gift of healing hands. I bet he even talks in tongues too. I don't believe in any of it. I don't really think he's a "true believer" either. If he was, he wouldn't have reacted the way he did towards the first sergeant. "Sure Mike. Anything's worth a try."

When he finally gets me home, Mom and Dad are off doing some errands. He helps me gather my gear; the same gear Mother hoped he would take off my hands, and sets it inside the doorway. He then lays his hands on my head and starts praying out loud, "Jesus, wonderful and just Lord.

Grant Jack this gift to be healed by your power." He then takes his hands off my head. "Do you feel the Holy Spirit?"

"Why yes I do," I lied to him just to get him down the road and away from me.

He leaves me and I struggle with my gear. He was right though, that was a waste of time.

On my days off, Mary has become my girl Friday by driving about to my doctors' appointments and waiting while I perform my physical therapy sessions. Len has also offered to drive me to work relieving me the added expense of monthly bus passes. Now that I have a more steady schedule where I'm working five days and off on Sunday and Monday, I can make plans on where I need to go and deal with what I want to do to get better.

The other day Frank wants me to get fitted for a new hand brace. I'm still dealing with the flat brace thing I had from St Luke's. Frank sends me to this place across from Holy Family Hospital. I'm quickly fitted with a hand brace that appears to work by bending my wrist slightly upward. I guess the point of this exercise is so my wrist won't drop and look palsied.

Of course, when I return to work the next day, pretty much everyone who sees me wants to know what happened.

"What do you mean?"

"Your hand; did you break it?"

"Oh that, no I got fitted with a new brace to keep my wrist from drooping down permanently."

Most appear to accept that explanation, but I think a few, knowing my recent history of falling down because I either lose my balance or my left knee locks up on me and I trip that way, thinks I broke my hand or wrist. Which, I sure, reinforces their belief I don't belong here. One day this older Filipino lady asks me when I'm going to retire.

"Retire? I'm only 44. I probably won't retire for at least another twenty years."

"Well, can't you collect social security?" She asks with her thick Filipina accent.

"No, I want to work. I can't pay my medical bills unless I work."

She thinks on this a moment, then states, "Well, I would do that. You deserve to retire, you work too hard as it is."

It's my turn to think on it before I reply, "I applied for disability, but was denied when I told them I planned to go back to work. Plus, they don't pay anything. I make twice as much working here than I could possibly make from social security."

"Oh, I didn't know that."

I wonder how many more think that way; that I could comfortably live on social security, and not have to work again. They probably heard stories of young mothers scamming the government out of thousands of dollars by being a baby factory. This Republican lie or myth, as you will, gets passed on from generation to generation. I'm sure it originated from when President Johnson signed all those welfare programs to offer a safety net for the extremely poor who can't live on what they make working. The Republicans oppose these programs because it fosters socialism and laziness.

It's Wednesday evening at the Moose Lodge, March 17, 2003. It's been advertised for days that we would invade Iraq on March 18, Bagdad time. There really is no surprise here. The major news networks have their crews reporting from Bagdad to witness first hand the shock and awe. I watch it all unfold with seeming disgust. Not just because our president is invading a country on allegations and innuendo, but because it's as if they need a scapegoat. I know this is wrong headed and will needlessly cost extensive lost of life on both sides. Iraq didn't invade this country on 9/11, terrorists from Saudi Arabia did. But, we can't invade them, they're our allies. Saddam Hussein is an evil dictator; a third point in the Axis of Evil that Bush described in his recent State of the Union address.

We watch in anticipation of the first smart bombs to hit their target, or the first cannonade of cruise missiles to reach the Presidential Palace inside the green zone. And then something strikes a building and a resounding explosion of flames light up the early morning sky. I see the lodge's secretary hugging a fellow lodge member, quietly happy we are at war against them. She is a cute fifty something with strawberry blonde hair that flows pass her shoulders. She wears glasses to see and her body is long and slim. It's quite obvious she was a very hot young lady thirty and twenty years ago. At this very moment though, I don't see her beauty. I despise her for wanting war and not caring that many American soldiers are going to lose their lives for no good reason.

I get up from the table I'm sitting at and move slowly over to the bar. I watch a group of four play a billiards game. The lady bartender comes over expecting me to order a drink. I don't want anything alcoholic. I'm thinking a root beer is my preference. She smiles at me, flashing straight white teeth. "I'd like a root beer, please."

"My pleasure," she exclaims enthusiastically. She goes to the refrigerator and pulls out a can and opens it. She then drops a couple cubes ice into a tall glass and pour three quarters full. I hand her a dollar as I stand at the bar and slowly sip my drink. "What do you think of this war?" The bartender asks.

I don't know her name. I'm not even certain that she's a member. I don't know what her reasoning is. I'm sure she probably thinks I'm a card carrying Republican that supports the President blindly and faithfully. "I think he's made the worse mistake of his career."

Her smile drains from her face as easily as if I'd slapped her. "How can you say that? He's an evil disgusting man that killed thousands of his own people."

"We're fighting the wrong person. Bin Laden is the enemy, but he's persona non grata. We can't seem to find him."

"Well according to our President, Hussein has been harboring terrorists and most likely has training camps there for Al Qaida. We're justified in every way in going to war."

"It's just a personal vendetta because he put a hit out for his daddy. He even admitted that a few months ago."

"What do you think?"

She suddenly turns her attention to a man sitting on a barstool next to me. He apparently has kept quiet on purpose; soaking in the point and counter point to the debate tasking place between the bartender and me.

"It's about the weapons of mass destruction he has stockpiled in bunkers all over Iraq. When we find those, then we'll be justified in going to war."

"I'm thinking if they find any weapons of mass destruction. Clinton and the UN stated that there aren't any more there."

"Clinton and the UN are a bunch of liars."

I see the hopelessness of continuing this argument. I learn long ago that never argue politics in a bar. I move over to the video golf game and play away from them and their fascination with their new hero whom they undoubtedly voted into office. I didn't vote for him. I voted for the other guy that should have been elected president.

I don't know if the events of 9/11 would have been any different under Al Gore, than under Bush. Most likely, it would have happened as it occurred. What I am certain on this day, is we wouldn't be wasting time and resources invading Iraq. My parents remain quiet about all this. I'm not certain what their thoughts are concerning this day in which the Bush Doctrine is in full fruition. Are they for it or against it? I'm thinking that they're torn between their own conservative ideology. They believe in less government. That's why they voted for Reagan twice. They believed in his belief that less government was preferable to what they perceived as Socialist liberalism that I tend to believe because I have that type of philosophy. But the Bush Doctrine, it brings more government intrusion into our lives. It created an entire new federal department and revamped the present bureaucracy to make it even more burdening. And they don't see any good coming from the Patriot Act. Neither do I. At best, it's flawed and needs serious tweaking. At worse, it's unconstitutional.

But I'm also certain they, like most American want to see our government do something that will show the world we aren't to be messed with. They're Roosevelt's children, who became empowered and mobilized for war after the Japanese attacked Pearl Harbor. The moment those terrorists killed the first flight attendant and took over the airline to fly it into the World Trade Center's North Tower, we were at war and it was retribution time. And I agree with that. We need to take out Al Qaida and other terrorists that dare to attack us and draw American blood. Invading Iraq is not the answer, and will cause serious consequences that we aren't prepared to handle.

The next morning all talk in the break room is the invasion. Its on CNN and Fox News. Like the Moose Lodge the night before, an overwhelming number are behind the invasion. The only casualty is a poor Marine tank driver, who's tank went into a pond or swamp, and he drowned. All indications are that it's a cake walk.

"Hell, while we're at it," opined a security guard, "We should just go and take out Iran too. Nuke them bastards. And let God find the innocents."

"We should," a slot attendant agrees. We got our troops there, we might as well do that."

I just keep my mouth shut because their opinions are just that, and I'm not going to lower myself to their level. The security guard I always find especially obnoxious. He always talks with that arrogance where Americans can do no wrong, and even if we did anything wrong, it's okay because we're Americans and the ends always justify the means. I hear him talking crap about Muslims. I tend to think he is the poster child for the ugly American. But I think that he wouldn't consider that to be an insult. Rather, he would wear that label proudly as a badge of honor. I can't listen to any more of his prattle and walk back to the Supply Room to wash ashtrays. But it doesn't mean I'm not thinking about what that idiot has said. It bothers me that people like that still occupy this planet in this day and age. Yet bigotry and jingoism is alive and well, and most likely will continue to be long after I'm dead and gone.

I remember that day so vividly too. I'm home getting ready to work. Mother and Dad have just left for work and I want to check out the local news. But, I noticed I'm running a bit late, and decide to leave instead.

The local radio station I listen to, is playing familiar hits. The dawn is breaking quite nicely, and I can see it's going to be a beautiful day. I get there in and there a quiet murmurings at the security podium that something is happening at the World Trade Center.

A few minutes later, while we're getting our selves ready to go out onto the floor, an announcement is carried over the PA stating a jet airliner has crashed into the North Tower of the World trade Center. Then, we witness on CNN the second airliner crashing into the South Tower. I'm in a state of shock. I know this is real; that it's happening in real time and that thousands of people are either dead or dying. But I feel numb by it all, like I felt when there was the explosion at Oklahoma City. At first I really thought it was a Hollywood stunt for a movie, and that Bruce Willis or Jean-Claude Van Damme would appear on the next scene of the trailer. It never happened though. Instead, see more images of the Pentagon building engulfed in flames as yet another airliner crashes killing hundreds more. And, finally word of another plane that crashed in Rural Pennsylvania, seemingly unrelated to the others, at first.

We watch in horror as the towers tumble into the street, killing hundreds more because there were first responders inside those buildings. Then we see images of the survivors leaving the scene, like the Israelites leaving Egypt in one mass exodus. Where they're going, I don't even think they knew. They only knew they had to leave what was The World Trade Center, and is now named Ground Zero to the safety of somewhere else.

At three o'clock we get word we're to meet at the flagpole. All flags nationwide have been ordered to half staff. Most of us that can get out from the floor are at the flag pole. It's quiet and done with utmost respect. I immediately stand at rigid attention and salute the flag as it is being lowered.

When we're done, we slowly make our way back to the floor. Some lady, who's vigorously playing her slot machine asks

Elizabeth what all the commotion is about. "We're lowering the flag to half staff for what happened in New York today."

"Oh, I don't care about them. I need a server to get me a coffee." When Elizabeth relayed the message to me, I just shook my head. This, I'm afraid is where our country has disintegrated to; selfish children who care for no one but themselves, even in a time like this. "I wanted to slap the bitch's face," Elizabeth stated.

"Elizabeth, she probably can't help herself. She probably has a birth defect; born with no heart."

"I don't care. Those are Americans that were killed over there." We're in our designated smoking tent that reeks of stale tobacco smoke and fresh tobacco smoke. There is very little ventilation and it makes a warm day feel even hotter. "Are you going over there?"

"Going over where?"

"To Arabia or Afghanistan or wherever that caused this today."

"Elizabeth, they're terrorists, they really have no country that they hold allegiance to. I'm sure, though, to answer your question, yes more than likely we'll probably be activated at some point and time as yet to be determined."

After work, my car radio's normal rock music format has been replaced by talk radio and news. All these people on the radio are searching for answers as to why we got hit like this. There are even those who see it a prophecy fulfilling, as they quote from Nostradamus and Revelations. And it doesn't matter what station I tune to, it's all about 9/11.

I don't make it home. I need a drink to get my mind off this. I arrived at the Wagon wheel to have one to several. But, it's all on TV too as Fox News regurgitates everything that's transpired over the past 14hours or so. There are no baseball games to watch in deference to the victims, baseball has been

119

postponed until further notice. Football is also put on hold. I'm left to sit there on my bar stool feeling hopeless and tired and becoming increasingly angry at all that has happened. Of course I blame the terrorists that did this, but obviously our own government's policies in the Middle East, from unconditional support for Israel, to our addiction to Arab oil, has much to do with what's happened to us this day. I go home feeling more depressed than when I came in here to "forget" about the day. Tomorrow's a new day after all.

It's the middle of April, and on a Sunday, when I get a call from Cathy. "Hey you. Guess who I just saw at the airport this morning?"

"I don't know. Who?"

"Dave Rodgers, Gus' brother."

Gus was a nickname for Loraine Rodgers, a girl I had a liking for in elementary and junior high school. She was the ultimate tomboy who was more at ease with her horse and playing flag football with the boys, than with going to the mall or playing dress up with the girls. I liked her spontaneity and her honesty. She had no problems telling it like it is, no matter who you were. The fact she was incredibly good looking and had a nice body with firm youthful breasts, also had a lot to do with my admiration of her. "He just got back here from doing her funeral; he said she died from breast cancer. Her funeral was yesterday. Sorry Jack, I know you had a crush on her in high school."

I momentarily caught my breath. I can't believe what I'm hearing. Gus is dead? But, I tried to put up my most manly voice, maybe expression, is more likely. "Wow that really sucks."

"David really looks good though. He's married and living down in California. I guess he's really successful. Anyway, I have to get back to work. Bye I love you."

I hang up the phone and go online to find her obituary. It's a short thing, probably hand written from her father, who I found to be a complete asshole when growing up. But, I guess when one is a head of household, one is entitled to be an asshole. She died surrounded by family at the hospice there in Kennewick. It doesn't say anything about friends though. I wonder if she truly had any friends. I wonder that with myself because of all the bridges I've burn to this point in my life. I know I have acquaintances, work colleagues, and former friends who used me. But, I don't really know if I actually have any real friends. I'm not certain I was Gus' actual friend. I would think, if we were, we most likely would have married and shared a life together. That obviously didn't happen.

It's Fourth of July 1985, when I see her on her horse riding alongside a young girl of six or seven that looks like her when she was that age. They're getting ready to ride the parade route for the West Richland Days Extravaganza. "Hey there Jack. How're you doing?"

"I'm okay. I've come to watch the parade . . . Mom and Dad are part of the Moose Lodge float. Is that your daughter?"

"Yeah, she's my pride and joy; always getting into trouble. I can't imagine where she got that from."

"Me neither," I laughed. It must be her uncle."

"Yeah, it must be. What are you doing these days?"

"I'm going to college at WSU, and doing the National Guard thing still."

"Well, I wanted to go to college after high school, but something else got in the way. Oh, I think we're up, Maybe we'll see each other later on."

"Sure, I'll be looking for you."

I never saw her after that. Either we just missed each other, or the next time she saw me, I was drunk or stoned off my ass, and she purposefully avoided me. All I know is what I'm reading here in front of me. She still had her maiden name, which means she never found the man in her life that would give her complete happiness. I can't see me being that man. The man that sired her daughter, obviously wasn't Mr. Right either. I don't even know if she married at all. Knowing her, probably not. The obituary doesn't elaborate.

I write an e-mail to Tamera on the news that Cathy conveyed to me from her TSA post at Tri City Airport. I don't know exactly what I feel right now. I'm obviously sadden by the news, but how close was I to her, really? I definitely wanted to be real close to her, but circumstances denied that from ever happening. Her circuit and my circuit never really meshed except for that one fateful summer day in 1985. I was too interested in getting drunk or stoned, or educated at a college, while she was busy raising a daughter by herself. Now her daughter has grown up without the one person that she truly counted on in her life.

I feel a twinge of emotion as I finish reading her obituary. I truly wish I could have been there. But, our lives were not meant to converge. I know I want a woman like Gus, though. I'm certain such a person exists. I'm not going to go out of my way to find her; that would be silly. I would suspect that she will come to me some day, and that I would know the very instant I see her, she would be the one. My secular god will help me find her, or, she will unexpectedly find me. Which ever, or how ever, is not the point here? What is the point, is my dream to find that woman to spend the rest of my life with. I don't know how much longer my parents have left on this planet. I can't afford to wait for that day when they are no longer alive. And I don't want to live my days alone and without someone to count on. And I don't want to depend on my sisters either. Cathy has her own family, and

Tamera is looking for a new life in Bend, Oregon. It's scary as hell. And the fact I have to deal with this stroke isn't going to attract the babes either. But, it might possibly attract the right person for me.

It's towards the end of May now. The unusually warm spring has given way to a early summer heat wave. I spend my off days at Phase One Physical Therapy trying to regain strength in my arm and leg. I probably rely too much on this quad cane, and not enough on trying to walk unassisted. I move about in the backyard hitting golf balls with my eight iron. I recently bought a net to catch the balls that I hit, but it seems to launch over the net and becomes lost. The dogs don't seem to mind since the extreme slices that come off the toe lands in their dog kennel for them to claim as theirs'.

During my physical therapy sessions, Frank has worked tirelessly to get my left leg strength up by having me do leg presses and squat thrusts on the leg press machine that utilizes elastic bands as resistance while I push the sled I lie on forward and back a certain number of repetitions. He has me lie on my belly, either on the bed or on a mat, and attempt to bend my leg. As far as my arm he makes me work my hand to grasp and a rubber ball. But, this is where I see my limitation. I see the ball and want to grasp the ball with my left arm, but it's like there's a wall or barrier between the wish to accomplish this task and my brain's ability to complete the task.

On my last visit to Dr Morgan, I discover an important reason why. She shows me my latest CT scan. On it, it's as clear as night and day; while the left brain shows a normal, healthy looking white, the right hemisphere is a dark void, as if a light switch has been shut off. I watch it in seeming disbelief. But, yet it must be. I'm sure some day, the left hemisphere will compensate somehow and allow me to use my left side in some limited manner. But, for now, my right side brain is dead, lacking the ability to use right brain functions and right brain tasks the left hand and arm requires to complete the total job.

On a Tuesday morning I am at work, but I don't feel my self. I took my meds like I've done these past six months. But today, I feel less than well. It feels like my stomach is doing flip-flops, and finally I locate the nearest trash barrel and puke my morning's breakfast in to the black lined can. I make my way to the to the EDR, but that really should have been the last place to go. The food odors makes me feel worse. I slowly sip on a cup of water, hoping that it will soothe my stomach.

Beverly sits down across from me with her plate of food. "Bev, I really don't feel well." I hope she gets the hint and leaves me alone, but she laughs at me instead, like I'm kidding.

"How you doing Jack? Are you done with the ash trays already?"

She has left over chicken on her plate, and I can't hold back the bile any longer. I release what contents, mostly water, are in my stomach. "Oh, Jack! Why didn't you tell me you are sick? I can't eat that now." She abruptly gets up and moves to another table behind me. I move out of the EDR and head back to the supply room to try and finish more ashtrays. But I can't. The smell of cigarette ash and the sight of butts is making it unbearable now. I just want to go home, but I'm trapped here.

Bob, the resident medic here, comes with me to the supervisor's office. Roger is on today. "Hey Roger, Jack is pretty sick and I think we need to send him to the hospital. I think he's has some sort of reaction to the drugs he's taking."

"I just want to go home, Roger." I tell him. I don't know nor care why I'm sick, I just want to go home. But, I'm getting the impression I'm not going home just yet. That, instead, they want me to go to the hospital first, which means having to take an ambulance there. That will mean another added expense. An expense I can ill afford.

"Well, Jack is there anyone home that can pick you up?" Roger asks.

"I don't know. Dad keeps a fairly busy schedule throughout the day. It'll be a crap shoot at best to determine if he's home. Plus it'll take several minutes for him to get here."

"I think you would be better off getting an ambulance to the hospital and getting checked out first."

"Is there someone I can call to get them to meet you at the hospital?" Bob asks.

"Yeah, get hold of Mother and have her meet at Deaconess Hospital. Here's her number you can reach her at." I hand it to him from my wallet. I see him pushing buttons on the keypad and waiting for the receptionist to answer the phone at Shiners' Hospital. When he finishes talking to her, he calls for the ambulance. Five minutes later I'm wheeled out the employee entrance on an ambulance Gurney, and so the rumors begin to fly.

The ambulance trip takes maybe fifteen minutes before we make it the ER. The paramedics do a battery of tests including checking my blood sugar. I know I'm not diabetic, but they just need to make sure. I'm wheeled into a room where Mother is waiting for me. I'm given some drug through my IV tube, and the nurse has me sign some form. The drug must be quite fast because I'm suddenly having a hard time focusing on signing my name. The last thing I remember seeing is another ambulance Gurney being rolled in as a paramedic is pumping the chest of a obese man, who I'm certain, is all but dead.

I wake up four hours later. Mother is there waiting for me. "You slept good. That left arm and leg was moving all over the place. I don't think your paralyzed. But, you do need to get that arm and leg exercised more."

The ER doctor come in and watches me briefly. "How long have been on the anti-seizure medication?"

"At least since my stroke. Is that the problem?"

"I don't know. It's possible I suppose. Anything's possible. I don't want to say one way or another at this point because the medication is prescribed to you by probably one of the best neuro-surgeons in the nation."

He looks young, probably an intern or first year resident, with thick curly black hair, dressed in blue scrubs and a testis cope dangling from his neck. I don't tell him he lacks a backbone. I just figure he's too young to make waves. "What we do now?"

"Well, I inform her what happened and that I temporarily took you off phenytoin."

I have my doubts that he'll accomplish that feat. But I'll allow him his fantasy. I have to go piss first, then I'm released to go home. I'd like to be a fly on a wall at Dr Morgan's office. I'm sure she'll dress him down to the point of utter humiliation, before sending him on his way with his tail between his legs.

The following week, I'm at this clinic where this doctor Mr. Morgan sent me has me hooked up to these wires pasted to my head. She ordered an EEG to measure my brain's activity. It's her contention that I'm very much at high risk to have a seizure, and I still need anti-seizure drug to keep me normal. I get the impression that she can't admit that she made a mistake. I've been doing much better without the phenytoin and know that was what caused me to get sick last week in the first place.

So here I am on two hours sleep over the past twenty four hours with these sensors attached to my skull. It's all very top secret; the doctor belays nothing to me as these printed out paper strips showing my brain activity is shown to the doctor. Then the nurse comes in to unhook me from the machine.

I call her again the following week, borrowing Mary's cell phone. "Dr Morgan's office, can I help you?"

"Yes, this is Jack Armstrong, I'm supposed to talk with Katrina about the EEG results."

"One moment please." I wait about two minutes when she comes on.

"This is Dr Morgan."

"Yeah, Katrina, it's Jack Armstrong. What were the results from that EEG?"

"Well, your brain wave activity still has me concerned enough that I want you to continue to take phenytoin for the foreseeable future. Also, have a primary care doctor yet?"

"Well, no I haven't."

"You need to get one. I can recommend a couple doctors for you."

"I guess I'm confused as to why I actually need a primary care doctor."

"The most important reason is I'm not qualified to be your primary care doctor, and I can't see you anymore. Second, is your need to have yearly physicals and I'm not set up for that. Lastly, you need someone that can give you all around quality care. I'm a specialist, not a general care physician."

"Very well, send me the names and I'll see what I can do."

A couple weeks later I receive her e-mail on the names of doctors to contact. Both are at the Fifth & Browne Clinic. I was hoping it would be further north, not in the shadow of the South Hill. I call the number and hear the receptionist's voice. "This is Dr. Morris voice mail, please leave your name and number . . ." I hang up on that note considering what's been going on with those yo-yos at Anesthesiologist Associates. I don't want to be playing phone tag when I need to see this doctor or discuss some medical problem over the phone. I try the next number.

"Hello," the receptionist sounds like she has an attitude. "This is Browne & Associates. What does this concern?"

I'm taken aback a bit by her tone. "Well, I've been referred by DR Morgan to get a doctor. I mean a primary care physician."

"What insurance are you under?"

"Premiera Blue Cross."

"I can get you in two weeks from tomorrow at 10AM. Is that alright?"

"I suppose it is."

"You'll need to come in twenty minutes early to fill out paper work, bring in your insurance card and have your twenty dollar deductible when you arrive."

I hang up after she does. What a bitch she is. I push her out of my mind and concentrate on getting ready to see Frank. Dad and drops me off Frank is outside enjoying the June sun when Dad pulls up to the Phase One parking way. Frank helps me get out his pick up truck. Then he walks over to the driver's side to introduce himself to Dad. For reasons I can only guess is the brown color of his skin, Dad reluctantly acknowledges him and in a half-ass manner, gives him a weak hand shake. I'm totally pissed at his racist attitude. I apologize to Frank.

"Don't worry about it. He's probably has something else on his mind."

Yeah, like why couldn't he find a white man to be his physical therapist? He refers to Martin Luther King as "that nigger." I don't remember him being this bad when I was younger. But, he always tended to keep his views to himself. Or, maybe he sensed I didn't follow in lock step with his political views, and didn't bother to speak out loud what he really thought. What ever the case, his outspoken racism has put us both at odds with our feelings for each other.

He's really shown these views in its full bloom when he suddenly decided to join the National Rifle Association ten years ago. I used to like this group because they were really big on gun safety and hunting training for kids. But then they became so politically involved in opposing legitimate gun legislation, regardless of what it was, that I completely disassociated myself from these people. They now believe people such as Hillary Clinton and Nancy Pelosi are the real enemies of America, not Al Qaida. I just shake my head at the ignorance of their demagoguery. I'm hearing talk that the NRA wants to place a constitutional right in the new Iraqi constitution like our second amendment preserving gun rights' ownership. I'm sure some time in the future such as a constitutional guarantee may well be warranted, but not right this instance when our military is trying to secure the peace there.

I can't think I'm to blame because Dad believes as he does. I'm sure his belief system goes way back to before I was born, but lately, he's definitely gone further to the right than even I thought possible. I don't know if he sees what I see. Maybe he does and his internal mental chemistry sees a totally different outcome than I do. I think him moving out here in the hills, presumably away from civilization may have more to do with his political shift than anything else. He doesn't have to accommodate anyone else's belief system. He doesn't have to be a good neighbor, and he hasn't been either. My parents' neighbors down the road from their house can't stand him.

It's on that note, when Dad found excuses for not wanting to take me to physical therapy, and I ask my neighbors to take me, that I ended up using Mary as the chauffeur for my appointments, that then leads me to my next goal that I'm attempting to accomplish; driving on my own again. It's not that Roger and Laura didn't care for me, nor that they weren't able or willing to help me out, they became really tired that Dad would allow them to do it when he's perfectly capable of taking me to these appointments himself. I could see where this would be leading and decided to nip it in the bud before I literally would be left in the cold.

After that day we went to fight our war against terrorism, a Lodge member asked me to referee a pool tournament the following Saturday. I obviously can't play any more, but certainly I could handle any challenge to the rules that may arise during a tournament.

"Sure, I can do that."

"Great, be here by six."

"I'll probably be here sooner since I'll just be coming in after work anyway."

"You work on Saturday?"

"Yeah, I work, but I'm off by three."

"You couldn't get Social Security?"

"I didn't want it. I feel if I'm still capable of working, I'll work."

"Well, I'm so proud of you, Jack."

It's not what he said, but how he said it that causes my reaction; as if I'm a complete moron or retard. "How's that?" I reply defensively.

I think he caught it; I hope he caught it. "Oh, well you know, that you would want to work, rather than accept government hand outs."

I know he's lying, but I let it go. "So you want me to referee a pool tournament? That's a first."

"It's done all the time where I'm from in Livingston, Montana." I didn't think I remember him from before my stroke. He reminds me of the character Grizzly Adams, big, tall and bearded. He seems nice enough, which is probably why I'm on my guard. I also feel he's trying to sell me something I don't want, and knows I'm vulnerable.

"Sure, I'll do it if Peter is going to be there because I'll need a ride back and he's the only one."

"Oh, yeah he'll be there. He was like the first one to sign up for this tournament." I think he sees my apprehension. "Look, I'm not trying to mess with you. I needed someone that knows the game and knows the rules. I know you fit that criteria quite nicely. I know you don't know me, but Peter and Mary have told me all about you and I trust their opinions. So. What do you say?"

"I said yes."

"Great, be here by six and the tournament starts at seven."

So it's Saturday and we are at the Moose Lodge preparing to do this pool tournament. I meet up with Peter and his wife, Jo Ann, a very petite red head with glasses and pretty smile. We share a table. Mary comes in and she sits at the buddy bar, a long table that sit around four and a half feet high that has bar stools surrounding the table. She signs up and deposits the entry fee to Bill. She comes over to me and we begin to talk of small safe subjects, then I ask her if she wouldn't mind being my personal assistant to take me on appointments.

"Not a problem Jack. Your Dad don't want to do it anymore?"

"Apparently not. I guess I'm cramping his style." I didn't want to delve deeper into his recent racist attitude toward Joel that left me feeling very awkward.

The following Monday the Mary era begins. Amazingly we get along a lot better than with Dad . . . Something to do with her being a pretty woman and Dad being Dad I suppose. "Basically, I'm hoping to get my license to drive again," I tell her on the way to physical therapy. "So, this is like really a temporary thing. Before Christmas I want to be driving my Intrepid legally."

"Are you saying you don't have a license?"

"Something like that; but I can explain."

"Please do, but when we get done with physical therapy."

The hour long session seems to speed by and we're back in her Mitsubishi mini van speeding away from there to home when I continue where I left off. "It all started in 1997 when I was convicted of DUI. The District attorney insisted upon throwing the book at me, and because my defense attorney was a piece of shit jerk, convinced I was wasting his time, wouldn't even help me appeal the conviction, I lost my driving rights. Then, while I was on National Guard annual training, I was called to court; when I didn't show up, a bench warrant was issued against me. Mother loaned me the money to clear the warrant when I got the job at the casino. Out of a matter of pride, perhaps, I refused to pay more than that, including going to alcohol school, and paying any of the fine."

"Looks like you will have no choice. Eventually, if you want to drive legally again, you'll have to do those things that the judge ordered you to do."

"I know, but maybe, if I wait long enough, they'll overlook most of the fine and maybe the alcohol school."

"Good luck with that."

"I know it's a long shot. But, what the hell, I need to at least try to skirt my responsibilities here." Mary gives me this side-long glance and smiles at what I've said.

"Jack, just pay them the fine and do the school and take ownership for what you've done. You'll get your license back sooner that way, than by the way your suggesting."

"That would be a first for me." Mary reminds me a lot of another girl I knew back in 1988.

We met at a tavern in the Queen Anne District in Seattle. I was living there to try and find quality work. My partner, Chester had invited me to live there at his place; actually it was his mother's place and it was a two bedroom apartment just up the block. She walked in and I smile at her and she comes up to me and asked, "My cat followed me down here. "Could you help me shoo her away?"

"Sure, I'll see what I can do. My name's Jack."

"I'm Mary Lee," she replied as she shook my hand. Her hand is warm and dry. She looks a lot like a younger version of Chloris Leachman. She had the pretty smile that was a pleasure to look at, Grecian nose that was long and thin, high cheek bones and pretty blue eyes, complimented by a full head of long blonde hair.

Her body was healthy and lean, like a dancer's. Her breasts seem a bit too small for my tastes, but her legs appear strong and athletic. I follow her outside and we find her cat underneath a car. "There you are. Why don't you go home, I'll be okay, this nice man is going to entertain me tonight."

"I think she'll be okay," I volunteered.

"I know, I just worry about her that's all." "Let's go back inside." We walk back in together and find a spot at the bar. I buy her a beer and we begin the conversation talking about unimportant topics that won't change the world dynamic. But it's important in getting some sense of what we're about. One beer leads to four more. We move from the bar to a booth. We talk some more about our past. I told her I had just turned 30 and was a WSU grad looking for work in Seattle as a writer. She told me she was a 39 year old Ad-writer for a local television station when her world came crashing down from a grand mal seizure she experienced two months prior.

We shot some pool and threw some darts and drank another beer before the bartender called last call and we walked out to her apartment together. It just seemed natural for me to be with her on that night. I probably wouldn't had bothered to ask her if I could spend the night with her, but I did.

She confessed she hadn't made love with a man in a couple years. I believed her and I confessed I hadn't for that long myself. We explored each others' bodies, her moles and my spider bite scar I got when I was three. We kissed for the first time as I removed her bathrobe off her shoulders to reveal her small breasts and flat tummy. She never had children.

I wanted to go down on her, but she said no, that for tonight she just wanted to be entered the "normal way." So I mounted her like the missionaries did years ago. She had Moody Blues playing as I moved in and out of her in time to the melody and drum beat. Then I climaxed. I don't know if she came that night. She stated, "You hurt me!"

"I'm sorry." I then rolled to my left side and fell asleep.

Three days later I called her to see if I could come over. She told me that would be fine and I arrived later that afternoon. She fixed me a dinner of Brussels sprouts. She had a noticeable limp. When I asked her about it, she stated she cut her foot on some broken glass the other night.

We made love together that night. The next morning she asked me where I was living. I told her the night we met, Chester's mother had the cops throw us out because he got pissed off about burning a dinner he was preparing. We were living in a hotel off first Street just down from Pike Street Market. "I'll tell you what, live with me, at least this month, so long you don't ask me to marry you."

"That's fine with me." I replied to her and sealed the deal with a kiss. For the next two weeks we lived together in, what I thought, was perfect harmony. But then on a Monday night, I stayed out way later than I should have, and didn't call her. When I arrived, she angrily let me in and stated in no uncertain terms, "I'm not running no damn flop house here. You need to take responsibility for your actions and call me when your going to hang out with your friends."

"I'm sorry! It didn't occur to me I had to let you in on every little thing I do. Besides, didn't you tell me you had a date with a lady friend and that you probably wouldn't be home until later?"

"That date fell through when I had to go to the clinic and get a glass shard taken from my foot. The one time I needed you, you were not there for me."

"I'm sorry I let you down," I stated earnestly. I came to her and hugged her and told her I may have a job moving furniture. We made love that night. She informed me she needed to get up in the morning to go and see her alcohol counselor.

The next morning would have been perfect, except she forgot to set her alarm clock and woke up way too late. "There's a bracelet I need you to get for me for this meeting." Try as I might though, I couldn't find the bracelet she wanted. This *only added to her frustration. Then her other boyfriend shows up to take her to the meeting. "Who the hell are you?"*

"I'm here to help Mary Lee find a bracelet for her." Of course I'm barely out of bed, barely dressed and barely awake. All he sees is a strange man in his girlfriend's house.

"Well you tell her she can find her own way to that meeting," and walks to his car.

She's just getting out of the shower. "What's going on?"

"Apparently your friend didn't know I was living with you."

"What the hell did you tell him?"

"All I told him was that I was helping you find a bracelet, which I still can't find."

"Shit! He wasn't suppose to know. Of course he left; a handsome man like you, and he's gone."

She gets dressed and goes out to where the bed is, and pulls the bracelet that she had me searching over God's creation for from between the mattress. "I hid it from you because I didn't trust you."

I really wanted to go up to her and slam my fist into her mouth. Instead, though, I said in exasperation, "I'm going to take a shower."

Later that same week, I received my first paycheck, and I bought her dinner and drinks at the same tavern we met. Saturday night I went with my boss and Chester to Spokane. Chester went back to Seattle, I stayed in Spokane another two months and never saw Mary Lee again. I wanted to. Three weeks later I came up with my boss, I think his name was Earl, to Seattle to check on his operation and I tried to call her up to see if we could meet up and catch up a bit. She answered the phone, I said "Hey there Stranger . . . How're you doin . . ." She hung up.

I remember other women in my lives. Most were young girls that I grew up with. Like my male counter parts, they faded into my personal history, never to be heard from again. Now I have a friend in Mary, who I like to spend time with from time to time. I don't think there's a relationship there. I don't see us as an item. I think she's a bit unstable, but so am I.

She appears honest and down to earth, like Gus was. I don't know though if I can trust her with every dark secret I've ever had, though. I'm not sure I should trust any woman with all of my dark secrets. I have some buried deep in the bowels of my conscious that I will never divulge to anyone. Only God knows of those secrets, and I hope He has forgiven me.

I focus on the here and now. Mary drops me off at Phase One and I work with Frank to increase my balance. He has me walking up and down steps with my quad cane. He has me lifting five pound weights from a machine with cables to hold the weights in place. He has me doing something called cariokas, an exercise similar to line dancing where I'm moving my lower body, cris-crossing my legs while moving laterally down a measured line approximately twenty feet. Another exercise he has me do is laying flat on my stomach and attempting to bend my left leg. Following this I move my arms above my head, in an attempt to stretch my arm and shoulder muscles. Then he has me move my where I'm in a crawl position, and I do a push up so I'm bending my arms down, then up. The exercises in and of themselves are monotonous and seemingly without purpose. I find, though that there is a lot of benefit doing these well rounded combinations that combine weight, aerobics, conditioning and cardio to give me the best opportunity to succeed. Then, Mary shows up and she sends me home.

I rest up a bit. Then, depending on the weather, whether it's hot, I go outside to shoot golf balls into the net I recently bought at Wal-Mart. This is about an hours worth. Being able to practice my golf swing—it's another workout I do at Phase One—seems to encourage my tone to calm down a bit more. I discover that, as long as I continue to exercise my left arm and hand, it seems to keep my hand more relaxed. It almost seems that my fingers can bend more; appear nimble and flexible.

Today Mary is driving me to the primary physician for my first appointment and physical so Dr Morgan can cross me out of her history. The appointment is scheduled for ten o'clock. I have the number memorized into my cell phone I recently purchased through a credit card offer I recently picked up. And it's a good thing I did too because just as we're at the bottom of Big Sandy, her left rear tire suddenly experiences a blowout. She safely pulls the minivan off the highway and gets out to investigate.

I follow behind her to get an idea how long it will be to change. "Do you have a spare?"

"I'm not going to worry about it. I'll drive back up to Mack's to get them to change the tire. Then we'll be on our way."

I maneuver myself back inside the van and call the Fifth & Browne clinic to let them aware what's going on. The same bitch answers the phone. "What's your date of birth?"

What does that have to do with the price of tea in China? "September 2, 1958."

"What's your name?"

"This is Jack."

"I need your last name too!"

"Armstrong."

"You have a scheduled appointment for ten o'clock."

"Yes, I know. I'm calling to tell you I'll be running late. We're experiencing minor mechanical problems."

"Well, just try to get here as soon as possible." She hangs up on me before could tell her how much a bitch she really is.

Mack's is a garage/gas station like it was before the Arab oil embargo in 1975. He don't have full service pump service, but he works on cars inside a two bay garage. It's one of those quaint little fringe benefits of living in a small village like Sun Crest. Mack greets her. "What's up Mary?"

"Got little blow out. You got a patch or an old used tire?"

"Let me see." He looks at the flat tire, then states, "I'll see if I can find a used tire that would fit." He goes inside the garage. A moment later he comes out with a tire that I can see is barely legal. He brings out a floor jack and places it directly under the rear axils. The entire rear lifts up. He pulls out the pneumatic wrench and loosens the lug nuts and removes the flat tire. Mack then places the used tire on the car. But the lug bolts are too big for the holes in the tire. So, he goes about removing the flatten tire from it's rim. He throws that tire away, places the rim off to the side of the hydraulic tire puller, then repeats the process with the used tire. Finally, he mates the used tire with Mary's rim. She pays him ten dollars for the tire and we're off to the appointment. It never fails, with me anyway, that whenever I'm in a hurry or running late, traffic lights are all turning red, and the slowest drivers are seemingly in the way.

We finally make it to the clinic, but then, naturally, we can't seem to find the clinic. I finally go to the pharmacy there at the Fifth & Browne complex to ask the person behind the counter where this clinic is.

"It's on the third floor, but you have to take the elevator, and it's confusing if you've never been there because it goes by a different name than what is listed on the Directory," the pretty pharmaceutical assistant or intern informs me with her winning smile.

"Thank you," reply as I make my way up to the elevator and push the button for the third floor. Sure enough it's on the third floor but the name is on the door mustn't have been changed to match the clinic's name. I walk up to the receptionist and inform her in my warmest voice, "Sorry I'm late. I have my insurance card right here." I hand it to her.

"Who are you?"

"I'm Jack, I called earlier to inform you I would be late."

She obviously isn't used to this kind of work. "What time is your appointment?"

"Ten o'clock, that's why I'm apologizing for being late," I reply evenly not letting my patience slip away and my temper take over.

"Here fill this out and hand it back. I need your insurance card to copy."

I hand her the card and take the clipboard with an application to be filled out. I sit down in a chair in front of the receptionist desk. It's like any other clinic's waiting room I've ever had the pleasure of coming to. There's the kid's area with the various toys and children's books scattered in a organized hap-hazard manner. There are various number of vinyl multi-colored chairs; I never understood the reasoning behind that that is placed next to each other. Since most people are more comfortable with there own personal space being 36 inches, it's odd that these chairs always violate that law of human nature. I always sit at least one chair apart from the person I'm going to sit next to, if I don't know that person. I quickly as I possibly can fill out the information. The receptionist keeps looking my way impatiently. I can feel her eyes on me, but I ignore her until I'm done.

I quickly hand her the form and she hands me another form to sign. "This is a privacy form, read and sign it please." She places the application in to a robin's egg blue manila folder. My name is already on the folder's tab and she places the folder on the organizer box to be picked up by the next available nurse. I read and sign the privacy statement and pass it back to her. I hear my name being called. The nurse, a thirty something blonde with imitation tortoise shell framed glasses holds my folder in her delicate hand. I hadn't sat down in the chair so I slowly move my way to her and the opened door.

"How are you doing Jack?"

"I seem to be doing okay. But I guess we'll find out soon how I really am, won't we?"

"That's true, we will." She leads me to a white room with white curtains. There's a padded table that she seems to think I can get myself up on. I prove to her right away that I can not. "Okay then. I'll also need you to put this gown on. Do you need help undressing?"

This wasn't part of the agreement. I hate taking off my clothes for the doctor's appointment, though this pass year I've pretty much loss all notions of modesty. "No, I won't need help. Do I need to remove my underwear too?"

"No," she replies. "That won't be necessary. Push this button when you're done." She points to a black button next to the room's light switch. Then she leaves. I dress into those white gowns with no back that have strings that normal people can tie in the back to help keep it on their bodies. I can't tie the back and it barely covers me. I push the button and wait seemingly forever for the nurse to return. I look at the Grey's Anatomy charts posted on the walls and door. When in comes the nurse followed by an intern. The badge reads Susan and she is short, petite blonde with deep blue eyes and perfect teeth behind a pleasant smile. I guess her age around 23 or 24. I bet she looks great in a bikini.

"Hi, I'm Doctor Susan James. How are you doing?"

"Hey there, Susan, I'm pretty good." I hand her a letter from Joel stating what has been going on from the physical therapy point of view. She briefly read it then goes to the form I filled out.

"Let's check your blood pressure first." She wraps my left arm with the blood pressure strap and pumps the rubber bulb until it's fully inflated and releases the air valve. I feel the blood pumping inside my arm.

"My goodness Jack. Your blood pressure is pretty high. Are taking blood pressure medication?"

I look at her. Doesn't that receptionist tell these people anything? "No. I can't believe you didn't get told, but I had a stressful morning. A lot of stuff happened and that's probably why my blood pressure is high."

It's obvious she doesn't want to hear the particulars of my morning. She probably didn't want to hear as much as I already told her. "I'll see what I can do about putting you on some high blood pressure medicine."

"You can do whatever, but as I already told you, my morning was quite stressful. I wasn't even certain I would make here at all." I could tell that these people are probably under contract with some big name pharmaceutical company to sell some quota of drugs for them. It's just another example why our health care system is so screwed up. These drug companies making the doctors treat the person's problems with drugs rather than try to figure out what probable actions or bad habits caused the problem in the first place. I already made up my mind to try and find someone else on my next physical exam. I definitely don't need their business. I don't care how pretty the doctor or nurses are.

The rest of the physical went without incident, and to be certain that it may have been a fluke, she rechecks the blood pressure one last time. This time, my pressure is well in my safe zone. "Your in good shape then."

"So do I still need to be taking that anti-seizure medication?"

"I don't think so. I'll let Dr Morgan know that I'm dropping you from the medicine she prescribed."

"Sounds good to me. I'll see you around then."

"Yes, of course. I'll want to see you again next month, in the afternoon. That way you'll have plenty of time to make it here and feel so pressured."

"If that's what you want."

I walk out of the exam room after getting dressed and set an appointment for next month with the one person I've decided is responsible for me wanting to take my business elsewhere. She doesn't smile when she sees me and I tell her I need a follow-up appointment next month. I want to tell her, "Relax honey, this will be the last time you'll ever have to see me." But I don't. Instead, I receive a slip of paper from her giving me the time and date. I then go down stair to the PAML clinic where blood is drawn to find any blood diseases. Once, I'm done Mary takes me to Phase One.

Frank shakes my hand firmly and asks how the exam went. I look at him with my most exasperated look and reply, "it was a nightmare. I don't know how that place stays in business. They are so disorganized and that receptionist is a total bitch."

He looks at me with a combination of mirth and unease. "How's your blood pressure?"

"I don't know. It's probably pretty high right now." He waves me over to the bed and I sit down while he opens a box and pulls out a blood pressure gauge to take my pressure. I want to protest, but know all too well that it won't matter here. I watch him do the procedure and he looks at the reading. A look of surprise crosses his face as he notices it isn't as high as he feared.

"Very good Jack," Frank states earnestly. "It's only 110 over 75. That is quite normal. I guess we can go ahead and get a good hour's worth of workout from you then."

It's early August now and I'm not using the cane anymore. I have a schedule to do the driver's test at St Luke's Rehab. I realize that what I'm doing is probably considered illegal because I am knowingly providing false information to the lady processing this case. I know why I'm doing this too. It's because I so much want to be independent, I'm willing to do about anything to be a licensed driver. It's the alcoholism that's affecting my judgment right now.

She doesn't know me or anything about me. She doesn't know I'm an alcoholic with a suspended license. I show her my state ID instead when she asks so nicely for my drivers license. She doesn't actually look at the plastic card that states right there that it is a State of Washington Identification Card. Either she chooses to ignore that obvious fact, or she is truly stupid. I hope she isn't stupid. I should just take the piece of plastic away from her and tell her to for get about it. I don't though. I don't because I'm so desperate to be my own person and be independent.

She gives me some tests to perform before we get on the road. They apparently are designed with the premise that a person who has had a debilitating stroke, wouldn't be able to perform these test with any confidence. I pass her tests with flying colors and we go outside to the sheltered parking lot. She has me get inside the driver's side and she screws a plastic knob onto the steering wheel. "What is this?" I ask without enthusiasm.

"Well, it's an aid in case you need it to maneuver the car quicker."

"I don't really think I'll be needing it, but okay."

"If you don't need it, I'll take it off. Do you know how to get to the old Costco parking lot?"

I quickly put my navigator helmet on and studied my internal map to get an indication as to what and where she is referring, I remember it from many years ago when Mother took me there. "Yeah it's over there on Third before it goes to the freeway."

"That's where I want you to drive me."

"Sure thing," I reply wandering why she would want to drive to a vacant parking lot."

Once we arrive she has me drive the car around the parking lot using that steering knob aide exclusively. I don't like it. I feel like a handicapped driver using it. Of course the entire car is set up with a handicapped driver in mind. There are levers in place in case the person driving, is a paraplegic or amputee. After a bit though, I disregard the extra contraptions and drive without noticing these things. I concentrate on the conditions around me. She gives me directions around the South Hill area. It's an area of Spokane I'm not used to. I've been to parts of the South Hill, such as around the hospital areas at the foot of the South Hill, and Grand Avenue.

Back in 1988, after my romantic fling with Mary Lee, I came to live in Spokane for a time. Robert hired me in Seattle to be part of his full service moving company. He told me he recovered from alcohol abuse. He said this to me while loading a bowl of prime Colombian green bud. He had the look of a hippy, reasonably long, but well groomed hair and neatly trimmed beard. He blamed his alcoholism on his felony conviction in California. He never told me what crime he was convicted, and I never asked.

I never told Mother I had moved to Spokane. I never thought I would be staying there over two months, like I did. I spent most of my time helping customers move their precious belongings from one place to another. After a bit, I became quite adept at driving about most of Spokane, including South Hill neighborhoods.

To the here and now I'm relearning this area. The streets themselves haven't changed much. There are a few more homes, apartments and strip malls now than before. The fact that she is also directing to certain neighborhoods that I wasn't exposed to back in my moving days back in '88, could also be lending to the confusion. Perhaps these neighborhoods didn't exist back then.

Or, perhaps these neighborhoods were not high on the full service movers' priority list back then.

I recall reading an article about an elderly man that drove his car into a crowd of people, and I asked her about that. "Do you think he had some reaction to the drugs he was taking?"

"I'm not sure. But I think he may have been too old to drive."

"Do you think older people need to be tested every year?"

"Well, maybe not every year. But maybe a more vigorous exam set up where other tests besides the normal ones they do."

"I think you're right in that regard. Give them the same type of exam one gets to earn their drivers license, plus a driving test."

"The problem I see with that, DMV are always so slow anyway. They would need to hire people to cover just senior drivers. Take a left here and get back on the freeway."

Mary sits inside her car as I arrive from the driving test. I realize I pulled the wool over this lady's eyes, but I'm equally certain I wouldn't be able to fool a cop should I get pulled over. I still have a suspended driver's license.

The next three days I drive my Intrepid, without Dad's blessing because he knows damn good and well that I'm not legal to drive. "I want that idiot's name," he told me the next morning when I pulled myself in behind the wheel of my car. "How the Hell could you pass a driving test when your not even licensed to drive?"

It all seems to be going off without a hitch. I don't recall being this tired though when I used to get off work. It's Thursday afternoon. I have the ac running as it is over ninety degrees today. I make it through Nine Mile Falls and see Lake Spokane lapping up against Nine Mile Falls Dam. The water is too low for it to spill over the spillway. I look at the lake quickly, with envy, as I drive on. Once outside of Nine Mile Falls, the speed limit gets back up to 50 and I accelerate accordingly. The highway makes a bend right at the Little Spokane River Bridge. I listen to the music playing on the radio. I harmlessly close my eyes for a second and the second is gone.

I feel a sudden jarring and my car is slanted up on my right. I open my eyes to see what the problem is and realize I'm not on paved highway anymore. I realize I can't correct my error now; it's too late. I ride it out. The car goes airborne for a moment, and then lands on soft sand, just missing a giant boulder that I'm certain would have caused the airbag to deploy and tore up my car real bad. The radio is still playing music, the air-conditioner is still cranking out cool air, but the engine isn't running. I try to start it back up, but it won't start.

Somebody is at my car door. I attempt to open it but something is blocking my door. I feel a bit dazed by what has just occurred. "Hang on," He yells. "There's a rock next to your door."

I wait as he and a flagger help move the rock out of the way. "It's okay, you're clear." I open the door and slowly climb out.

"Can you help my pull my car out? I seem to got myself stuck."

He looks at me, and then the car. "Dude, you're not going anywhere. Are you okay?"

"Well, sure all things considering, I'm quite well." I walk over to my back door and pull out my quad cane. I move to the front of the car. It's bleeding out coolant at a rapid rate. Obviously, even if I could get the car started, I would be hard pressed to get it home. I may have even bent the frame. The turn signal on the driver's side is dangling from the front. The Good Samaritan just disconnected it and threw it in the back seat and closed the door.

The flagger that helped move the large rock out of the way, is doing traffic control, moving the gawkers and rubber necks along while we wait for whomever to arrive. Finally, a State Trooper pulls his white Crown Victoria near where I did my swan dive. It's a fairly steep bank that he maneuvers his six foot five long and sinewy uniformed body down to greet me. His uniform, though designed for summer, appears hot and uncomfortable. He wears his grayish blue Smoky Bear hat proudly, his dark sunglasses protect him from the sun, and conceal his identity. Once he makes his way down towards me and the Good Samaritan, he greets me.

"Well, what happened here?"

"I guess I got a little too close to the bank," I replied

"So I see. I'll need your driver's license, proof of insurance and registration, please." Thus the moment of truth as I reached into my wallet and handed him the State ID card.

I think he thought I am being funny. "You don't have a driver's license."

"No," I reply honestly. "I had it suspended in 1997."

I'm sure he had more questions than I could give him answers to. Like the car sales man, the loan agent and the woman at St Luke's who all overlooked the same piece of plastic as a mere technicality. I'm sure that am the tip of the iceberg here. I don't know about the rest of the state, but here it seems every time there is an auto accident, the person at fault has no license and no insurance. I'm sure he's thinking "here we go again." I did find the registration and proof of insurance in the glove box. At least all I'll get ding driving on a suspended license.

"Let's go up to my car. We'll call in a tow truck and I'll get your license thing straightened out." I fear the worse, that I'll be arrested for the suspended license. I move along the bank until I'm close to where the trooper's cruiser is parked. Just as I'm about to get in, Mother shows up and sees the result of my indiscretion.

"What the hell happened Jack?"

"Well, I got into a little trouble with this bank."

"Are you his Mother? The trooper asked.

"Yes I am. I can take him home now if you like."

"No, that won't be necessary. We have to wait for the tow truck first."

About ten minutes later, Dad shows up, parks his truck just in front of the patrol cruiser and places a safety cone there, and begins to direct traffic. "Who is that?" The trooper asks.

"That's my Dad," I reply with shameful embarrassment.

"Well, he can't be in the way like this. Hey Sir, that's not necessary. We have everything under control."

"Okay, if you think so. Where's my son?"

"He's okay; he's sitting back here out of the sun and heat."

He walks over to where I'm sitting, on the shaded side of the car with the door partially open. "I'm okay Dad."

"I told you that you aren't ready. I'm half tempted to get a lawyer and sue that idiot that said you could drive."

"Okay sir, why don't you and your wife go ahead and head home. We just gotta wait for the tow truck and he'll be coming home shortly."

Dad, seemingly reluctantly picked up the cone and threw it in the back of the truck, got back inside the cab and drove home. I heard radio chatter and finally his call came over. "I got your copy over. Yes, that's correct he stated he had a suspended license. Roger."

"It looks like you don't have a suspended license anymore. You will have to renew and complete whatever requirement that the judge ordered you to fulfill to get your license back. I'll cite you then for leaving the roadway and no valid license. You also are lucky that this happened here and not a quarter mile further up, since that's where the county line is and you would have to drive all the way to Colville to see the judge."

The tow truck arrives about an hour later. He apparently lives in Suncrest too and was told to do this job and he could go home. It took a few minutes to hook up my car and pull it from the embankment. Then both men help me get into the cab of the two ton tow truck that has a cab that sits way high.

"Where do you live?" The driver, who introduced himself as Eric, asks.

"I live off of Whitmore Hill Road."

"Well then, we better get there then." And off we drove to home with a disabled car in tow.

I can't drive without a license anymore. I thought I could, but it's apparent, since my stroke and the type of drugs I have to take, that driving is more perilous than ever. I thought I could drive without problems, but I'm having a hard time staying awake long enough to go anywhere safely. Am I destined to not being able to drive again? I'm sure I will eventually, but legally.

A few weeks later I'm dropped off at the county courthouse in Spokane it's sunny and breezy; Mother drops me off at the courthouse entrance on Broadway then she goes to find a place to park her Cherokee. I stand near the hotdog vendor's cart. I know I'm in for a workout. It's a very expansive campus, where the original court house stands, then the annex, that was built when the original building became too small for the county's ever expanding needs, and the county prison that is built like a skyscraper, but with narrow slats for windows. The Spokane Police and county sheriff share a portion of the annex.

Mother finally arrives and we walk together up the sidewalk steps and onto the campus. We begin our search for the traffic court and actually find it fairly easily in the old courthouse, on the third floor. We had to do the post 9/11 scanner search to make sure we weren't armed with guns or bombs. So we have to remove all metal objects from our pockets and place everything into a Tupperware dish send it through a conveyer belt type scanning machine and we pass through a metal detector. I beep off because of the metal on my leg brace. "Can you take that thing off?" the nice deputy asks.

I look at her with a sense of exasperation. "Can't you just wand me?"

"Yeah, I suppose we can do that." Another deputy steps up and runs a wand type scanner over my body briefly. "He's clean," he tells her.

We make our way to the elevator and end up at the court room marked three. The place is crowded with people caught doing something stupid with their car, including myself. The room is historic and antique. The benches, if they could talk, would have a myriad of tales to tell of the butts that sat there witnessing historic crimes and punishments that occurred over the past 130 years. I see four rows of benches, two columns deep. The juror's box is empty. No twelve angry men will be hearing any of this nonsense today. A long table sits where a clerk will be recording the proceeding. She busies herself with minor chores to ensure the afternoon session will go with out a hitch.

Normally, two other long and narrow tables would be occupied with a defendant and his attorney on the right and the prosecutor would sit on the left. And finally the podium where the judge sits, and just to his left is the witness stand. Behind the podium is a door that leads to the judge's chamber.

It seems to always take ten minutes longer than the prescribed time on the docket before the judge finally comes through the door. A deputy announces "All rise, Judge Gaylord Proctor presiding."

The judge is older and probably close to retirement. He has a bald pate and a well trimmed white beard and mustache. He appears thin and tall. "Everyone raise your right hand and repeat 'I swear to tell the truth; the whole truth; so help me God.'"

We all in unison follow his lead. Once we finish he orders us to be seated. I hear a lot of excuses for doing all sorts of stupid stuff. Dr Stannick's PA sent me a letter she wrote concerning my condition, so figure that would help a least lower the fine a little bit. I didn't read the letter, so I figure it would exonerate my action. My turn and I go ahead and try to explain to the judge what happened and that I have a letter from Dr Stannick's PA.

"I'm not interested in reading your letter. That would probably get you in more trouble if I did. Fine is leaving the roadway and creating congestion and operating a motor vehicle without a valid operator's license. You can plea guilty and pay the fine of sixty five dollars, or plead not guilty and it would go to trial where you can gather defense witnesses, including your PA, and let the wheels of justice take it's course. I would warn you that by pleading not guilty, you run the risk of not only paying a higher fine than you will by pleading guilty, you also may be charged court costs. How do you wish to plea?"

It is apparent as soon as he told me that he wasn't interested in reading the letter, he had my interests at heart. He would have read that I was under medication and fell asleep while driving home from work. I would have been charged with a DUI and probably have gone to jail again, had my license privileges revoked, and paid an outrageous fine of several thousand dollars. "Guilty," I replied without hesitation. We left the courtroom and paid the $65 fine.

Of all the things I've missed the most since my stroke is the simple pleasure of fishing. I so enjoyed going to a river bank or lake shore, even to get into a boat, bait a hook, and cast a line out as far as I could. It was always very rewarding for me, since I most always caught a fish or two. I never over fished either. To me, I found it wasteful to go after more fish than I was willing to eat. I missed that, and being able to golf like I used to back before my stroke. I last golfed I scored a 93, my lowest score ever. Then, two weeks later, I became half paralyzed. I don't believe I'll miss National Guard, though. It seemed that the more I tried to get promoted to the next level, someone was just as determined to keep me where I was. I know I could do the job, and did the job it for Lieutenant Art.

I'm certain he and others believed in me, but there was always someone else who considered me unfit. Those people have their own opinion on who or what a leader should be, and apparently I didn't fall into that pigeon hole. I just wish Lieutenant Art was still here; I still miss him.

June 3, 1999 and I'm at Yakima Training Center, on the tank gunnery range. My tank is in position to begin our tank table eight gunnery exercise. It's a live fire exercise. It's quite warm, but slightly breezy. Lieutenant Art's tank has been ordered to move into position. Then . . . "November, November, November," Sergeant Clark announced in a high pitched, almost panic stricken voice over the tank's radio and into my ear piece. We have an accident on Lane Alpha, I need medics here now. I repeat, there's an accident on lane Alpha, I need medics NOW!"

There's an eerie silence and I wonder what happened I can't see anything because I'm in my gunner's seat and sop dictates I put the main gun in the UP position because of a cease fire action being played out. Finally, Sergeant Berg tells me to go out and stretch my legs. It feels like it's been about twenty minutes since the cease fire action has been in effect. I still can't see what's going on at Lane Alpha. It will be much later in the day when I here the complete story. I look at the distant sound, moving closer; a familiar sound of rotors beating. The helicopter approached and lands at Lane Alpha, as a green smoke grenade gives the pilot wind direction. Five minutes later, the Blackhawk was back in the air seeming flying out at full throttle, mere feet above the ground, slowly gaining altitude. The chopper will be in Yakima in about ten minutes. I quietly prayed for whomever was hurt would be okay. "Sergeant, come back here. We've been ordered off the range, Sergeant Berg tells me. I get back in my gunner's seat next to the 120mm main gun. The driver puts us back on the tank trail that leads us off Lane Bravo. He stops in front of a safety NCO, who climbs on board to ensure the main gun and the machine guns are cleared. It's Sergeant Crafts, who was Lieutenant Art's acting platoon sergeant the previous year, when I was acting tank commander. He doesn't look right.

"It's Lieutenant Art." I look at him blankly. "Take off your helmet!" I do as he told me. "It's Lieutenant Art." I don't know what to say. I don't know if he expected me to say anything. I felt numb, but knew I needed to see my former company mates. Once the tank was parked, I pulled out from the gunner's seat, out the commander's hatch, and gathered my web gear and k-pot. I see Sergeant Quagmire talking with Sergeant Berg and the other two crew members on our tank. I jump down off the deck and hit the ground moving smartly towards Alpha Company's assembly area. Sergeant Quagmire follows me. "Hey Jack, can I talk with you?"

"Yeah, I know Lieutenant Art got hurt."

"I'm afraid he didn't make it. He's gone." I don't know what to say. I cry on his shoulder instead. "What the hell happened?"

"The driver was going too fast, tried to turn on to lane Alpha, went out of control and flipped the tank. Lieutenant

Art didn't have a chance. It rolled on top of him before he could respond."

Three days later the battalion gathered our tanks in a perfect square. The sun was slowly moving down the western horizon. We stood at attention, observing the pair of dusty combat boots sitting on a black cloth draped table, a color guard stood at attention as the American flag and our regimental flag hung limply in the center of this square. I can't remember what was said on that hot, arid evening. I just remember taps being played by two buglers, the honor guard firing their rifles over the silent air, and the Sergeant major calling roll and the name, Tom Art going unanswered.

I don't know what will happen to my brigade, since they'll be going to Iraq next year. They'll be leaving here in October, and won't be back until some time in 2005. I figure they'll have to do something that will be a complete waste of time. They need Engineers and Ordinance personnel more than infantry, artillery or armor. Somehow, the war has shifted from liberation to occupation, and the Iraqis are pissed. I just hope my Guard brothers don't end up in body bags.

It's early December; a full year since my stroke and it's been a long journey to this point, but the story is unfinished. It's been a year of sobriety and being clean from smoking cigarettes. It's been a year of relearning my work, rediscovering my own self and reinventing my worth to society. I called Mary to see if she could come over to wrap Christmas presents for me. Even when I had full unhindered use of my left hand, I couldn't wrap presents worth a crap. They always looked like I wrapped them wearing mittens.

"I also have something to show you Jack."

"Okay, I'll be waiting for you." I don't know what it is, but figure she's sending me gift too. I bought her a special gift and hope she likes it. I like our friendship where it is right now. I remember back in June or July, I had just finished seeing Dr Stannick and she innocently asked me where next. "We could go to a motel room."

She gave me this look of daggers flying at me, like she really wasn't in the mood for such nonsense. "Just kidding," I smiled at her, but the mood was unchanged. I think it was a matter of respect more than anything else. She was pissed at me because I showed her a lack of respect by throwing something at her that basically demeaned her and made her less than human. I was trying to be funny, but she didn't see any humor in it. I recognize now that we do have a special friendship that will never change. It's a friendship based on mutual trust and respect, and a sexual relationship can never be put in the mix to screw everything up.

She arrives and the dogs are barking. They bark because they like her. It's a friendly bark saying, "Hi, see us! Tell that ass hole sitting in that warm house to come here and let us out." She gets out of her van and I answer the door to let her in. She goes to the VHS player and explains to me as she places the cassette into the slot, "The wagon wheel is changing owners. Peggy is no longer running the place. She sold it to these people who will turn it into a Mexican restaurant." She changes the channel and the satellite is shut down, and the video is playing. "I put this together as a kind of time capsule to remind everyone about the people that went to the Wagon Wheel. I want to get your take on it while I wrapped your parents' presents for you."

"I also got you something too." I go to the stack of presents and pull out a velvet jewelry box. "Jack, you didn't have to get me anything." She immediately opens it to reveal a friendship bracelet. She hugs and kisses me on the lips. "Well, so much for what I was gonna get you."

"What was that?"

"I was going to have sex with you."

I'm sure I gave her a look of shock and surprise because her response is a quick girlish laugh and, "just kidding" reply like I gave her six months ago. I kiddingly sock her in the arm and then turn my attention to the video, that shows an assortment of videos and still pictures of the people in the past. It was a montage of the history of a tavern in Suncrest, Washington. Only the people who actually experienced the history would appreciate it. Any other outsider would most likely consider it quaint, or a complete waste of time. The last image on the video was one taken of me. I don't recall when that was. I just see me looking at me, a very sad and pathetic looking man very much alone in the world around him. I decided right at that point I would remain sober because I didn't want to be that person in the video again.

END